This Game Called Love

A Boston Love Story

By

Tana B

D1518382

Synopsis

Eighteen-year-old Teyanna 'Tey' Hunt is smart, beautiful, and a real catch. Any man that she allows in her world would be a fool to let her go, and Rico knows that. Even though she has broken it off with Rico, her abusive ex-boyfriend, he won't let go. Rico believes that Tey belongs to him, no matter what she says.

Terrence 'Terror' Mack, Brooklyn's bad boy, has money, respect, and power, so he feels he has it all. He doesn't realize he's missing anything until he lays eyes on the beautiful Teyanna. Terror decides right then and there that he has to have her.

With all she's been through with love and the crazy ex-boyfriend still threatening her life, Teyanna isn't in a rush to fall in love again, but Terror is too hard to ignore. His charm and swag demand attention, so it's not long before Terror is between her legs, claiming her as his. Once Rico finds out, does Tey still feel like a chance at real love is worth the gamble? Unbeknownst to Tey, one of her friends is really an enemy and is on a mission to destroy her happiness at all costs. With new beef brewing in the streets, a target is now on Terror's back, and anyone standing near is surely about to take the hit, and that includes Tey. Trouble is coming the couple's way, and they find themselves in a game of survival. With so many predators after the couple's happiness, is survival even a possibility?

Table of Contents

Legal Notes

Prologue

Teyanna
Two months earlier

J sat in the packed courtroom as I listened to the judge's ruling. "Sixty days and a fine in the amount of one thousand dollars," he concluded, banging his gavel.

You would think I would be heartbroken that my boyfriend was going to jail for two months, but I was actually relieved. This was a clean getaway; a new start. Truth be told, I hated Rico. The man I had grown to love over the past two years was of no existence anymore. Instead, a man who looked identical replaced him, but his personality had done a complete one-eighty. Every chance he got, he would degrade and belittle me.

I was tired of him fucking other bitches behind my back. Bitches were constantly wanting my head over his ain't-shit ass. I was tired of him putting his hands on me. I mean, I wasn't no punk bitch, but I was no match for him. No matter how much I pleaded and cried, he wouldn't let up. I'd just turned eighteen, and I had my whole future ahead of me. I knew I didn't deserve this, but what could I do? I was stuck.

I couldn't be with somebody who wanted to steal my debit cards or constantly accuse me of cheating even though I'd been nothing but loyal. Enough was enough, and after a year or so of agony, I got the sign I'd been praying for. I was too scared to confide in anybody. What would they think of me? Was I really that dumb? He made sure to put on this charade in front of others like we were just happy and everything was peachy, but I was miserable, and I wanted out.

Later that day...

"You have a collect call from... Rico, an inmate at Norfolk County Sheriff's Office. This call may be recorded or monitored. The cost for this call is three dollars

1

and twenty-five cents for a total of thirty minutes. To accept this call, please press zero. If you do not wish to accept this call, please press three or hang up."

I wanted to just block the call, but I needed to get this off my chest once and for all so I would no longer have to deal with this bullshit. I pressed zero and waited until he spoke.

"Damn, it takes you that long to answer my calls? What the fuck was you doing?!" he barked.

I couldn't help but roll my eyes before responding to his ignorant ass.

"Hello to you too, Frederick," I said as I laid on my bed. I was fresh out the shower, and all I wanted to do was crawl under my blanket and sleep. I had school the next day. I was in my senior year, and there I was dealing with this black, unworthy piece of shit.

"Yo, cut the shit, Tey, dead ass."

I heard him getting pissed. In that moment, I did'nt care. I felt like jail would protect me from him, so I decided to talk my shit, and, if anything, deal with the consequences later.

"What shit are you talking about?" I asked dryly, like I had better things to do, which I did. This nigga had treated me like scum at the bottom of his shoe for so long. It was time for some payback.

"Wassup witchu, my nigga? I ain't been in here a good five hours yet, and you already acting the fuck up. I swear to God, when I come home, you gon' see."

I honestly didn't care too much about his empty-ass threats, because two months seemed like long enough for him to forget. At least, I hoped it was.

"What are you threatening me for? This is why I can't do this anymore, Rico. I'm not your punching bag, and hopefully, when you get out, you'll find a girl and move on with your life," I said in one breath.

It seemed like the silence that followed was deadly. I knew he was still on the phone because I could hear him breathing.

"Yeah, my nigga, whatever. You ain't going no-muthafuckin'-where. I don't know what the fuck you thought," he said, laughing like I was telling some sort of joke.

The thing was, I was dead serious, and I was gonna prove it.

"I don't love you anymore, Rico." I spoke lowly.

I still lived at home with my parents. They had no idea what the real Rico was like, but they accepted him with open arms. He even worked with my dad a few times to get money. I can't even tell you how many times I had to cover up or lie about busted lips, swollen jaws, or black and blue bruises on my arms and legs.

On numerous occasions, my grandma Hannah, God rest her soul, would try to 'warn me' by telling me that Rico seemed 'too clingy' and it 'wouldn't be easy trying to leave a guy like him.' I knew what she was right, but I was too stubborn to admit it,

2

and I believe that's a big part of why I ain't tell anybody. I didn't want them to have the satisfaction of being right. None of my girls liked him, except Eboni. She actually introduced me and him. At first, he was the good guy who spoiled you with time, affection, and gifts, but then that all changed. He would always find ways for me to stay at his house so he could watch me and make sure I was 'being loyal,' and even then, that wasn't enough.

"That don't matter. As long as I love you and I'm happy, we together." He sang 'together' and began to laugh hysterically.

I felt disgusted. His voice, his face, and his whole being made me sick to my stomach. As stupid as it sounds, a long time ago, shit like that would make me happy. When he would get jealous and try to dictate everything I did, I would feel like he cared and that was his way of telling me. I thought it was because he loved me so much and was only trying to keep me to himself.

"Why can't you just leave me alone and let me be happy?" I felt the tears building up on the rims of my eyes. I wasn't a weak bitch, but I was exhausted physically and was mentally broken down. I couldn't take it anymore.

"I love you to death, girl. I ain't never letting you go," he said.

A chill went down my spine— not in a good way, though. I honestly felt like he would kill me instead of letting me be happy with the next man.

I should just kill myself and get it over with.

That thought disappeared as soon as it entered my mind. I wasn't about to tap out and give up that easily. I'd rather leave him and die trying to live and love freely than live the rest of my life in fear of constantly getting my ass beat.

"You have sixty seconds remaining," the operator spoke.

I was relieved because, as soon as the call was over, I was going to block Rico and get rid of any and everything we had. He was no longer what I wanted. I stayed to keep him happy, but it seemed like me being with him fucked up his mental even more.

"I'm blocking this number, and I think it's best you don't try and contact me anymore. I wish you the best, Frederick." I fidgeted my fingers, and my leg shook uncontrollably. I tended to do those things when I was nervous or pissed; in that case, I was both. I was glad the phone disconnected before he could respond.

Once the call ended, I placed the number on the blocked list and put my phone on silent. Afterwards, I lotioned my body, slipped into my pajamas, laid down, and tried to get comfortable enough to fall asleep.

No matter what side I laid on, it felt like I was lying on needles. The conversation with Rico had me up thinking. "Love me to death," I said aloud to myself. Maybe I was thinking too much, but I felt like I should leave at least until Rico wasn't thinking about me anymore. Did I think Rico would kill me if I ain't wanna be with him? Absolutely. But what could I do to get myself off that dangerous roller coaster ride?

Chapter 1

Teyanna

"*M*iddle fingers up, put them hands high. Wave it in his face; tell him, boy, bye. Tell him, boy, bye, boy, bye. Middle fingers up. I ain't thinking 'bout you." I was singing along to Beyoncé's new song while driving down Blue Hill Ave with my main chicks Taj, Lauryn, and Eboni.

We were on our way to this cookout-basketball tournament they were having in Tent City, which was located on the south end of Boston.

"Yo, sis, you think your boo, Jah, gonna be there?" Lauryn teased.

"He's not my boo; plus, he in jail again," I said sternly, emphasizing the word 'again' while looking ahead. You see, Lauryn is my big-mouthed best friend— well one of 'em— and we basically grew up like sisters; we are the closest.

Lauryn was beautiful, no doubt about it. She was five feet five inches and had the prettiest, most flawless brown skin. She had a fat ass and the deepest pair of dimples that she decided to have pierced. My home girl was gorgeous, and no one could tell me differently.

Taj was just as bad. She also stood at five feet five inches. She was mixed; her mother was white and her father was black. She rocked her curly, natural hair, had small boobs, a tiny waist, and a big ol' cornbread-fed booty. Not to mention, she had long, pretty eyelashes and dark brown eyes. She also had a few tattoos that decorated her body.

Eboni was the tallest out of all us, standing at five foot nine inches, and was skinny as a toothpick. She didn't have no ass and barely any titties, but she ain't need all of that. My baby still looked like a supermodel. She was mocha colored with hazel eyes and kept her hair short in a blonde pixie cut style.

And last but not least, me. I stood about five foot two inches. Short? Yeah, I know, but I had long, jet-black hair that reached the middle of my back. I also had my round button nose pierced and deep, chocolate brown skin. Not to mention, I had slightly chinky, chestnut-colored eyes and full, juicy lips.

So you see, I was a bad girl, and my friends were bad, too. We'd been tight since elementary school and nothing had changed.

My thoughts were interrupted by Taj and Lauryn complaining that they were hungry. We were too uppity to eat at a cookout with people we ain't know.

"Let's go to Flames," Eboni finally spoke up. Flames was, hands down, the best Caribbean restaurant in Boston.

"Girl, bye. We all the way on Tremont Street, and you talking about some Flames?" I huffed and began to laugh, shaking my head. We had just picked up Eboni since she lived here in Roxbury.

"Come on, Tey. Please, I'm starving," Lauryn cried out, trying to lay her head on my shoulder and look up at me with her puppy-dog face. I cut my eyes at her and refocused on the road.

"I'll even pay you gas money," Taj added, offering her two cents.

"Ughhhh, fine." I made an illegal U-Turn. Those hoes were lucky I was hungry too.

Fifteen minutes later

"Thank you so much, T. I promise I got you as soon as I get change," Taj said, hopping out the car and running into the restaurant, which I parked directly in front of, thank God, 'cause it was usually packed.

I made sure to check my surroundings. We were in Grove Hall, which wasn't the safest neighborhood. Niggas usually got killed or robbed up this way, so the faster we got our food, the better. I locked the doors to the black-on-black 2009 Honda Accord that I kept in mint condition. I mean it wasn't brand new or nothing like that, but it was mine.

Upon entering the restaurant, my mouth started to water as my nose caught a whiff of the food. I began eyeing all the different stuff they had, but I already knew what I wanted to eat as soon as we started driving up here.

"What are you getting?" the lady with the fucked-up teeth and the personality to match asked.

"A large peppered steak with rice, peas, and cabbage," I called out. It was really beans, but people from the Caribbean get easily offended or some shit when you say beans instead of peas.

My phone started ringing. It was Rico calling, yet again, from a private number. He had gotten out a couple weeks early. I'd been avoiding him at every chance I got. Lauryn was behind me, looking at my phone, and she spoke up once she saw me decline it.

"Ewww, what that nigga want?" She sneered. She knew it was him without me having to tell her. Lauryn hated the ground Rico walked on. She ain't sugarcoat it either. It was raw and clear-cut with her. That was why I loved her.

"Who?" Eboni asked while getting her change back from the lady.

"Nobody," I stated quickly, trying to defuse the situation before it even got started.

"Girl, who else? That whack-ass nigga, Rico," Lauryn spoke up.

I rolled my eyes and sucked my teeth. I didn't like when she put my business out. I was very private when it came to relationships and other shit going on in my life. I just wished others would respect that.

"He still on you? That punany must be good," Taj laughed. The rest of the girls joined in, but I didn't see a damn thing funny.

Rico made it a point to stalk me and sneak up on me too many times to count. To be honest, I was still too ashamed to tell everyone all the ugly shit about that insane-ass dude.

"I honestly don't want him. That nigga is crazy and sick in the head. He's been calling me for the last three weeks from a blocked number, and I can't block a number that I don't know. I blocked his number, his mother's number, and anybody I knew that was affiliated with that man." I was so stressed out because that psycho nigga still ain't catch the hint to leave me the fuck alone.

"How do you know it's him?" Eboni questioned while staring down at her phone and typing.

I rolled my neck at her. What she said pissed me off. It seemed like she acted dumb in the head when I explained, not too in depth, some of the crazy shit he would do, and she would make smart remarks and say sly shit like, "What did you do to make him act out that way?"

Maybe I was bugging, but it seemed like she was always trying to justify his craziness and place the blame on me. Sometimes, shit would make me question whose friend she really was. From my understanding, they weren't even all that close. They just knew each other.

"Obviously, I answered the phone and heard his ass begging and crying for me to give him another chance," I said as I made my way over to the counter to pay for my food. I just hoped she would shut up and drop the situation before I said or did something I would regret. Lucky for her, she took heed and kept her mouth shut.

Don't get it twisted, Eboni is still my girl, and I love her dearly. But it seemed like, lately, she wanted to get under my skin by judging me, and I wasn't down for that. She hadn't had a man for a minute, but she would try to give me advice. I had way too much going on, and her and her sly comments were getting to me.

Before I knew it, we were all piling back into my car and peeling back into traffic, loving the summer breeze, and jamming to Beyoncé. Soon, we were in Tent

City, looking for parking before I said 'fuck it' and double parked, blocking in a dark grey Rolls Royce.

"Uh uh, bitch! You better quit playing before they fuck around and tow your shit!" Lauryn yelled at me.

"They ain't towing shit. Come on and get out. I probably won't be here long, anyways," I said, turning the car off and taking the key out the ignition before stepping out.

Lauryn looked at Taj and Eboni in the back seat, and they just shrugged their shoulders and got out the car on my side since Lauryn hadn't moved. I finally heard her say, "Fuck it."

Niggas were tryna get a minute of our time left and right, but we ain't slow up not one bit. We knew we were slaying shit and were turning niggas' and bitches' heads. Well, Eboni's simple-minded behind tried to be friendly and entertain these no-good-ass niggas. The rest of us knew better.

To be honest, I wasn't feeling anybody. I mean, niggas did look good, though. I saw a group of 'em balling up on the court, and I they looked good as they ran up and down the court with no shirts on. I was 'bout ready to pass the fuck out, and most of those niggas had gold rope chains on like they were in a fucking video or some shit. Had a chick like me thinking about giving one of these dudes the time of day, but I wasn't pressed for money.

My mom was a social worker. My stepfather owned the best construction company in Boston, and my real father was somewhere in jail; I'd never really met him. I had a job and income of my own. It wasn't much, but it was still a job. Not a lot of females my age had that, so I was grateful.

"Oh, my gawd, bitch! Look who it is!" a random ratchet shrieked to her friends. She looked dingy and dirty as fuck with her hair in a weave ponytail that was off color from her nappy, dry, natural hair.

"Who?!" one of her friends said while puffing on a blunt. She didn't look too bad, but her clothes looked too small, and she had this aura about her that screamed 'hood rat.' She was a yellow chick. Her hair was medium length, and she had piercings and tacky tattoos thrown all over her body, excluding her face.

"It's Terror, bitch. Look," the first friend said, turning her friend's head to the direction he was in.

My nosey ass turned my head as well, and I must say, I was in awe. I saw what those hoes were so hype about.

"Bitch, I thought his fine ass lived in Harlem still?" the third friend asked. She was a little on the heavy side with cheap-looking clothes on and had an ombre-green weave that looked like it had been in forever. They all were looking at his ass like he was some type of god or something. Me, on the other hand, I kept it cool, but, on the inside, I was damn near ready to pass out.

"He do, but you know he come to the Bean every so often, tryna rack up and double his profit," the first one whispered to her friend. He wasn't paying any of us any mind, though. He went to dap up his niggas on the court and some that were standing on the sidelines.

"Girl, you see this fine-ass nigga?" Lauryn pulled me in and whispered in my ear. Lauryn knew better. Her ass had a whole boyfriend. Nas was off at Duke University on his basketball shit, but I knew my girl. Though she still loved to look, she was crazy about Nas and wouldn't give no other dude the time of day. On the flip, he was my godbrother, so I guess I wouldn't see too much of her flirting or being all up in the next nigga face.

"Yeah, he's a'ight," I said, trying to play it off. I pulled out my phone while trying to switch my mind onto something else.

She touched my forehead with the back of her hand, and then did the same with my cheeks as she looked at me like I was crazy. I looked at her, dumbfounded; we both knew I was lying.

"Baby girl, are you okay?" she asked. "Because that nigga is foineeee. God bless his DNA. If I was you, I'd get on that. He look like he got money," she finished up and made small talk with the rest of the girls as they agreed with her.

He looked like he was mixed with some shit. My guess was Puerto Rican or maybe Dominican.

He was caramel colored with a strong jaw line, deep brown eyes, and long, pretty eyelashes that were not too feminine. His hair was in a curly bush on top of his head. The nigga had the nerve to have the newest gear on: a red, short-sleeve, rugby Polo, some dark blue True Religion jean shorts, and a pair of red and black Retro 12s. Not to mention, his jewelry was laced; he had some big-ass, one carat diamond earrings, about five chains that shined extra bright under the sun, and a big-ass Rollie on his wrist. The nigga looked like money.

"Yo, who the fuck car is blocking me in? A nigga can't get out!" he yelled. He looked frustrated.

Everyone on the court's eyes were on him.

"Yo, Ock, what kinda whip was it?" a dude by the name of Guwop called out. He was one of the scariest niggas to fuck with— a certified street bully. I knew to keep my distance.

"A two-door Honda or some shit," he answered, grilling a few niggas in the park.

Lauryn and I shared a quick glance. I was too scared to speak up, so we stood up together, and she called out, "It's ours."

I was glad she did it, 'cause my ass probably wouldn't have said shit. He looked between the two of us, and his face softened a little.

"Can you ladies move it, please? I got somewhere to be," he requested in a tone way different than the one he'd had about ten seconds before.

The hood rat bitches glared at us like they wanted to catch these hands because I'd blocked in their so-called man.

"Of course," she said, smiling as she grabbed my hand so I could go and move the car. Taj and Eboni were close on our heels and having a small convo amongst themselves. Once we got to the car, he jogged up behind me, lightly tapping my arm.

"Ayo, ma, what's your name?"

I stood frozen. I didn't know how this tall, fine-ass nigga had me losing my words and shit. I was kind of embarrassed, but seeing him up close, borderline invading my personal space, I couldn't help but get a little tongue-twisted.

"Her name is Teyanna, and I'm her sister, Lauryn," Lauryn said, speaking up for me before I could make a total ass of myself.

"Is that right?" he asked, glancing from her to me and eyeing me up and down while licking his lips. He stood about six foot three inches with an athletic build. I swear, I wanted to faint. I even felt a little tingle down there, if you know what I mean.

I looked at him and nodded. "Ye-yeah."

My stuttering made me want to slap my hand over my forehead.

He held his hand out, I assumed for me to shake. After extending my hand, however, I learned that I was mistaken. As he took my hand into his, he brought it to his beautiful, even-colored, juicy lips and kissed it. Lauryn had already gone to sit in the car, but, knowing her nosey ass, she had seen the whole thing.

"Nice to meet you, ma. I'm Terrence, but niggas call me Terror," he said, smiling at me and slowly letting my hand go.

"Nice to meet you too, Terrence." I smiled before looking away.

"I'll see you around, though, beautiful," he said, walking off to his car where an ugly, light-skinned bitch that everyone called Red was sitting with an ill mug on.

I turned back around to my car, floating on cloud nine, with the biggest smile until I realized that Terrence was probably dating old girl in the passenger seat. Unfortunately, all the fine niggas were cuffed. Just as soon as the thought of me feeling him came, it got canceled. Terrence wasn't the type of dude for me. He was on a whole 'nother level.

I would have to find somebody else to help me get over Rico.

Chapter 2

Eboni

"*I* just don't understand why you keep calling this bitch! Like, what the fuck does she have that I don't?!" I screamed through the phone at the person on the other end of it. Not hearing a response from him pissed me off more, so I kept going. I knew he was getting tired of my bitching, but he had no choice but to listen. I was sick and tired of putting my feelings on the back burner.

"I'm the one in love with you. Why can't you just leave her alone?" I sobbed. At this point, the tears were flowing like a river. The phone call wasn't going well at all, but I was tired of that nigga's shit! I could hear him take a deep breath, but he ain't say shit, which had me piping hot.

"Hello! Hello! RICO?! Why aren't you saying anything? I'm tired of you playing me for this black bitch!" I continued to cry, finally fed up with the constant lies, broken promises, and worst of all, disrespect.

"Look, E," Rico said, taking a dramatic pause before he continued. "You forcing it. I'm not playing you for her. I told you I ain't want that broad! I'm tired of you always pressing me about this bullshit. On my dead dawgs, you're really starting to piss me off," he finished.

I had to look down at my phone because that nigga had lost all of his mind.

"I'm forcing it? Piss you off? I'm pissing you off? You know what, nigga? I'm the one dealing with this bullshit, and you could care less. But I'm pissing you off? Fuck you, nigga!

Lose my number," I snapped, shaking my head in disbelief.

Click.

I had to hang up before I really got disrespectful and said some shit I would later regret.

He always tried to play me like I was stupid. But maybe I was. Teyanna had been my friend for a very long time— over ten years— but I had always felt a twinge of jealousy toward her for as long as I could remember, even before she got with Rico.

I had been attracted to him since we were youngins. Nobody had a clue I was fucking him on the low before they even got together, but she just had to come along and take him from me. I kinda felt like she knew I liked him, and, in a way, I feel like she messed up my chance at falling in love and finding true happiness. Don't get me wrong, I loved my girl in my own weird way, but she just always had to come along and outshine me. I hated it!

She had the best of everything, including clothes, shoes, and hairstyles. On top of that, she always had the cutest boyfriends. I might sound fucked up for saying this, but the moment I found out they were together was the moment I vowed to ruin their relationship and make him mines by any means necessary.

Only problem was that he was really in love with her, and I just didn't understand why. In my opinion, I could treat and love him better than she ever did. Of course, he had some fucked-up ways about him. Like the fact that he cheated on my girl throughout their relationship, and he also had a problem keeping his hands to his fucking self, which she thought I didn't have a clue about. I, on the other hand, felt as if it was gonna take a real bitch to hold him down, and maybe he would see somebody was down for him and loved him, and then he wouldn't have to put his hands on me to make me understand or listen. Plus, we shared a secret so dark not even his precious little Teyanna knew, and we both planned to keep it that way.

Knock, knock, knock.

My little sister, Kiana, switched into the room we shared. She knew to knock just in case I had company over. She was fourteen and too grown, if you asked me. We lived in Ruggles Street Projects in Roxbury. It was me and my three siblings, plus my mom and her crackhead husband, who I could not stand for the life of me. My sister and I shared that tiny, cramped-ass room while my mom and her husband, Harry, stayed in the one across the hall.

My brothers, Harry Jr. and Zayvion, who were twelve and nine, stayed in the living room on the pull-out sofa. So there goes my family broken down for you.

I hated it there, and as soon as I got enough money saved up, I planned to move the fuck up outta that scummy-ass city, and I was cutting everyone off except my Rico. I even hoped he would say 'fuck it' and come with me. We could start a new future together, because, trust, I didn't think anyone would approve of our relationship.

My grandparents still didn't approve of my mom's relationship, for that matter. She and Harry were sixteen years apart, and he was her third baby daddy. The nigga was two years younger than my grandmother. He had no respect for anyone in our family and made it a point to dictate who my mom was allowed to see, which was only his nasty-ass family.

She was so lost. You would think she had a backbone, but it seemed like that crackhead nigga could steal whatever and sell it to get his fix, and she would take him back with open arms like a weak bitch. That couldn't have been me, and I put that on my granddaddy's bones. A nigga would never have me that gone, or so I hoped.

Chapter 3

Rico

"FUCK! I'm tired of this bitch, bro. I'm bouta let her go, on everything, my dude!" I complained while taking two long pulls of the strawberry-flavored Swisher Sweets blunt that was filled with the sticky-ass loud I'd just copped. I was trying to relieve some stress, but the more I thought, the harder it was. I sat back in the seat as I watched Teyanna's ass leave her job, walk across the street, and slide into her car. She had my head all the way gone, and she knew that. Even though she swore up and down she wanted nothing to do with a nigga after all I put her through, I wasn't letting her go. She was mine 'til one of our caskets dropped. If she didn't get with the program, it would be hers.

"I been told you that, nigga, but nah! Yo' slow ass keep fucking with the crazy-ass bird after she lied about those two pregnancies and about keying your shit. You need to get your fucking mind right, my nigga," my little brother, Jermaine, preached. I sat there, taking in everything he said for a few minutes, and made up my mind. Eboni wasn't nothing serious at all, but let her tell it, we were. See, ya boy was fucking with Eboni way before Teyanna, but once I laid eyes on Tey, I had to have her.

I even cut Eboni's looney ass off for a bit, but she was like a stray cat that kept coming back, plus her pussy was type moist. It was like that shit kept calling me back.

"I'm done with her, bro. For real this time!" I vowed while pounding my fist on the car's dashboard.

"Yeah, a'ight, nigga. I'll believe it when I see it. 'Cause you said the same shit not too long ago, and you still entertaining the bitch," Jermaine said before pulling into traffic.

I let my mind wander as we followed a few cars behind Tey. I just wanted to know she hadn't moved on to the next nigga before I stepped to her. Even if she did, I'd end up killing him and claiming what would always be mine.

Later that night

Boom, boom, boom.

"Who is it?" I heard Eboni say through clenched teeth.

I was already annoyed; she knew it was me 'cause I told her to have that pussy ready and that I would be there in a few!

"You know who the fuck it is. Open this fucking door!" I barked before waiting until she did. As soon as she did, that dumb bitch had the nerve to start swinging on me.

"Fuck you! Fuck you! Fuck you!" she screamed over and over again while punching me in my chest.

"Ayo, chill the fuck out," I warned, restraining her arms and overpowering her.

Still, she wouldn't let up.

"Yo, for real, E, you need to chill the fuck out before I beat the shit outta you! This why I'm done with yo' crazy ass; you always being fucking extra. I'm tired of your shit, too, bitch! You can't do shit for me. You can barely do shit for your own fucking self, but you always hollering about holding a nigga down. I don't need you!" I barked at her.

She saw the seriousness in my eyes and knew that it was best to keep her hands to her fucking self. I turned and tried to leave, but the constant tugging of my arm caused me to turn back around. I watched her wipe her eyes. Seeing as how she knew I wasn't moved by tears, I knew she was about to start pleading her case.

"No, baby, please! I'm sorry, baby. Don't leave. I'll make it up to you," she hinted, licking her lips and tugging at my Ferragamo belt buckle. Her brothers were on the futon, sleeping, or so I thought, but I ain't give a fuck. Her moms was working overnight, her step-pops was somewhere sniffing his brains out, and her sister was asleep in their room, so she dragged me into the bathroom. I ain't object because I wanted to get a nut off and be out.

"Come over here and bend over the sink," I commanded upon entering the bathroom. She locked the door so that there wouldn't be any interruptions in the small, cramped bathroom. I unzipped and pulled out my eight-inch schlong, and she eyed my dick hungrily while watching me stroke it as it got harder. I was about to put her ass in her place.

As she assumed the position and spread her legs, I decided to fuck with her head a little. I started playing with her pussy, making her coo and moan out loud. I spread her ass cheeks as wide as they could go, so I could get a full view, and rammed my dick right into her ass, making her yell out in pain. I ain't even bother to lube up either.

13

"Shut the fuck up," I said harshly, biting my bottom lip as spit flew from my mouth. Before I knew it, I was choking her from behind with one hand and covering her mouth with the other, making it nearly impossible for her to cry out.

She choked and gagged into my palm between her low sobs. I ignored it and sped up my pace. She tried to reach her hand around to push me off her.

I was tryna go balls deep.

"Move your hands before I snap your neck." I removed my hand from her mouth as I roughly grabbed her jaw and spit in her face.

"You like that, bitch?" I chuckled sinisterly. Once I felt myself building up my nut, the tip slowly beginning to ooze pre-cum, I grunted, pulled out, and came on her back and ass.

Tears streamed down her face. I looked down at my dick, which had blood, cum, and a little bit of shit on it. I grabbed a clean rag and cleaned my dick off while looking down at her ass in disgust. When I was done, I threw the rag at her as she cried silently in the fetal position on the bathroom floor.

"Clean yourself up and shut the fuck up with all that damn crying! Damn. You almost made my dick soft," I laughed. I was gonna stay and get some pussy, but she'd fucked all that up already.

After unlocking the bathroom door and walking out, I made my way out the door, not bothering to ask if she was okay. I ain't have time for any of that bullshit. I had plans on making that money and getting my wife, Teyanna, back.

Once I got back downstairs, I went to the back parking lot to get my whip. It was damn near midnight, so I wasn't worried about anybody seeing me. I grabbed my keypad out of my back pocket and unlocked the doors on my 2011 Dodge Charger. Once seated inside, I sparked a blunt and twisted the key in the ignition before pulling out my phone and taking a couple pulls of the blunt. I had five missed calls and about the same amount of texts. I decided to call my cousin, Mace, back and see what the fuck he wanted.

"Ayoooo," that annoying nigga answered.

"Woooo," I responded, looking around at my surroundings. The hood wasn't safe; niggas would kill you for walking funny around there.

"What's good, my nigga?" he asked, being nosey and questioning me like some hoe-ass nigga.

"Nothin'. I'm around, though. What's popping?" I asked, wondering what this nigga wanted.

"My nigga, I'm tryna pop out. That nigga Terror out here, and I'm trying to see if he gon' put a nigga on," he said, dick riding while I continued toking, not really giving a damn.

I'd heard of Terror. Who hadn't? That nigga was basically on his way to running the east coast's drug and gun games, if he wasn't already doing so. I just wasn't on that nigga like everyone else. I would have rather had my own shit and not be following after some nigga like a hoe, but Mace was hungry and wanted to get put on. Me? I would have bodied that nigga, taken his place, and ran the streets. I would just have to be prepared for his goons and everyone else coming for my head.

"Alright, my nigga, be outside in about twenty. I'll be there," I finalized the call while reversing out of a parking spot and driving in the direction of Hyde Park, where he lived.

∞ ∞ ∞

Once I pulled up less than fifteen minutes later, I was in the mood to peel the fuck off and go back to Eboni's. This dumb ass nigga had the nerve to have niggas with him. I wasn't feeling that.

See, that was one thing I didn't like about my cousin. He had a big-ass mouth and loved to be flashy about shit. I mean, ain't nothing wrong with flaunting every now and then, but be smart about the shit. I had a feeling he was around those niggas when he was talking about linking up with old dude.

"What's good, my G?"

He said, getting in the passenger's seat and holding his fist out to dap me up. I left him hanging as I watched the funny-looking cats he was with try to open my back door without acknowledging me. That only intensified my anger. I turned back with fire in my eyes.

"Ayo, who the fuck is y'all niggas?" I looked between the both of 'em. One of the niggas was short, chubby, and black as hell with a gap between his two front teeth. The other nigga was tall and goofy-looking. He kinda reminded me of a younger version of Snoop Dogg.

"Hey, whaddup? My name KK, and this my right-hand mans, Shake," the tall, skinny one spoke up with his hand out for me to take.

I looked at his hand like it had germs or some shit before turning back around in my seat. I glanced at my cousin while putting my car into drive.

"Next time, come by yourself, my nigga. You know how I feel around strangers," I said, making sure them niggas heard me and daring one of them to check me. I pulled off and went in the direction of our destination. I was heated, but I planned to stay cool, calm, and collected until one of those muthafuckas jumped stupid. Then, I would let that cannon bark.

Chapter 4

Taj

$\mathcal{R}$eentering my room after taking a much-needed shower, I grabbed my phone off the nightstand. I had a missed call and a few texts. I saw a few from my girls, Lo and Tey. I didn't really talk to Eboni much anymore. I only hung around her 'cause of Tey. Other than that, we were cordial. She could probably tell that I didn't like her, but quite frankly, I didn't give a flying fuck. She seemed sneaky as of late.

I saw that my baby had called and was probably wondering why the fuck I wasn't answering. I called back while I played with my naturally curly mane that was pushed up into a bun. My light-blue towel was wrapped tight around me. I waited impatiently. I was just about to hang up until the voice I'd been dying to hear picked up.

"What?!" she answered.

Yeah, you read that right. I dated a female, and we were happy. Her name was Regina. We'd been together for a little under nine months. At first, I wasn't even interested in her like that, but it happened. We fell in love and had been unbreakable ever since. Both of us had tried dating guys, but we never felt that spark like when we were with each other. It was unexplainable.

"Come on, Pookie, don't be like that. I was in the shower. I called you as soon as I got out," I tried pleading through the damn phone with her stubborn ass. After about thirty seconds of silence, she sighed and responded sweetly.

"Okay, babe, but I miss you."

I could hear her pout through the phone, which caused me to smile 'cause I knew she couldn't stay mad at me for long, no matter how hard she tried.

"I miss you more," I responded, trying to sound sad as sad as I felt. I wished we could be open about our relationship. Gina's family knew she was bisexual and that she was in a relationship with me.

My family, on the other hand, didn't have a clue. My father was a deacon at Faith Christian Church in Dorchester, which meant he was a very religious man and didn't play that homosexual stuff. It was an 'abomination'. I knew I would eventually have to tell him, but I wasn't ready to then.

My mother and I barely kept in touch. She was a junkie that traveled from state to state, doing only God knows what and with whom. Last time I heard from her, she was somewhere in Arizona.

However, my stepmother, Danielle, whom I loved and adored, had been there for me since day one. When I was six, I was taken by the state because my mother had left me and my infant sister, Hailey, in the house alone for two whole days.

There was no food in the house. By the time they found us, we were dehydrated. Good thing I was smart enough to call 9-1-1 after one of my mom's angry customers came one night, banging and yelling at the front door about burning the house down if she didn't give him back the money she'd stolen.

"Wanna sleep over tonight?"

"Uh, I don't know, babe. It's kinda late, and you know how my pops feels about me sleeping out," I said somberly. My dad was strict and didn't let me go out past nine-thirty at night, even in the summer. I would have to beg and clean or something to get him to say yes.

"Come on, baby. Can you please ask him? Please? Plus, your dad likes me. Tell him me and Mommy are coming to pick you up or something. I'm sure I can walk a couple blocks up and meet you," she said.

"Okay. Fine. I'll be there. Just gimme like twenty minutes, and I'll hit your line when I'm on my way,"

"Yay!" she cheered. "Okay, baby. Love you, and I'ma get dressed now."

"Love you too," I said before pressing the end button on the gold Galaxy S7 Edge my step-mom had gotten me for being on the honor roll for the whole school year.

I had just graduated from high school a few weeks earlier and could party for a bit without having to study twenty-four seven. I was my step-mom's future nurse, she always bragged, maybe even doctor if I stayed dedicated.

She and my dad had no children together. She *did* have a daughter named Olivia. Notice: I said 'did.' Olivia would've been around the same age as me, but she died from drowning after having a seizure in the bathtub. We were the best of friends, something like sisters, my dad and her mom informed me. Also, they had a son together named Quinton, Jr., but he had died after three months in the NICU. When he was born, he had a hole in his heart the size of a quarter. Instead of closing, it opened wider. That was when I was about eleven.

After a while, they gave up, and I believed that was why they babied me. Danielle had been the only mother figure I had most of my life, so I called her my mom. I admired her strength. After losing two children, she never stopped loving and caring for me.

"Mom! Dad! Mom! Dad!" I yelled, walking out my room and down the hall toward the stairs.

"Natajah Renée Carter, I know you done lost your ever-loving mind!" my father said. He walked into the foyer and looked up at me standing at the top of the stairs.

I smiled and pranced down the staircase. "Daddy, can I stay at Regina's house tonight? They're having a girl's night and—"

He put his hand up to stop me.

I was going on nineteen, but my dad didn't give a damn. His house, his rules, as he would always remind me.

"Natajah, do you see how dark it is? Look at the time. It's darn near midnight." He sounded so funny trying not to curse, but I couldn't laugh, because his tight ass would probably say no.

I made a sad face and kept begging until he caved in and gave me forty bucks to order pizza and stuff. He wanted me to go straight there and call him so he'd know I was safe. He wanted to drive me, but I was quick to tell him I was meeting Gina halfway. He was serious when telling me no boys, but I assured him he had nothing to worry about.

Walking out the house with my bag of overnight clothes and personal items, I dialed Gina's number up as fast as I could. I took slight right off the street, putting a little pep in my step.

"Hello. You on your way?" she answered on the third ring.

"Yes, babe, I'm walking to your house now. I should be there in the next five minutes." I looked around the dark streets at the multiple cars and buses cruising by. We lived in the hood, so I had to be extra cautious just in case some niggas tried to act stupid.

"Alright, sexy, I'll see you when you get here. I hope you ready," she purred seductively.

I blushed and playfully rolled my eyes while wrapping up the phone call and trying my best to get there as fast as I could.

Within seconds of entering Gina's room, she and I were all over each other. I was the first to break away from our hot and steamy kiss. I couldn't help but admire her beauty. Her hazelnut complexion, short, black hair that she kept in a mushroom cut, greenish-gray contacts, and long, pointy nose stood out to me. Not to mention, she had one of the most beautiful video vixen bodies I had ever laid my eyes on. She had double-D cup breasts, a tiny waist, and a booty that, if I didn't know any better, I would've sworn was fake. She was all mine. That was an added bonus. We were two bad bitches in a fem-fem relationship. Most guys would have been in heaven if we went that route and allowed a man into the bedroom, but we were both selfish.

She stripped down to her birthday suit and started undressing me, practically ripping my clothes off.

Once my last article of clothing was removed, she began sucking on my nipples. She moved one hand to my nice, round, plump ass and the other to my fat, soaked kitty. Throwing my head back in satisfaction, I parted my lips and let out a slight moan. Regathering myself, I lifted my head and started kissing on her neck.

Gently pushing me onto the bed, she took control again. She took her time licking and sucking on my hardened nipples.

I cried out in pleasure, which made her look up at me with her devilish grin. She traced her tongue around my belly button a couple times before going lower. Finally, she buried her face into my ocean of love, licking, sucking, and slurping on my clit like it was the juiciest fruit she'd ever tasted.

I couldn't take anymore. I exploded for the first time, but that didn't stop her from feasting.

"Pooh, *stawwwwppp*." I tried to push her head away, but she gripped my thighs and pulled me closer.

"Oh, my fucking gawd!" I shrieked as I continued to roll my hips, creaming in her mouth a second time.

She drank up all my juices and came up with a big-ass smile. I was drained, and we hadn't even gotten started yet.

I sat up and rested on my elbows as she went under the bed and pulled out the blue-and-white Adidas box that held about six dildos. We decided on one together: 'The Rabbit.'

I laid her down and grabbed the strap on piece after sliding one finger down her slit and watching her body shiver in pleasure. I giggled and leaned down, placing my lips on hers.

"I love you," I said, slowly sliding the dildo inside her.

She gasped as her eyes rolled to the back of her head.

"I love you too," she moaned out while placing the vibrator on my clit. She bit on her bottom lip while I rubbed our noses together and placed a passionate kiss on her lips.

Chapter 5

Teyanna

"It's over!" I exploded in tears. "I can't deal with this anymore," I said, getting off the bed to escape his room.

I was tired of him and all the extra shit that came along with with him. I wanted to see if he really had changed or if this was some half-assed way to keep me wrapped up in him.

He laughed and stood in front of me, blocking me from leaving. I knew going over there with nobody else home was a bad idea, but he said he wanted to talk about us. I didn't know what it was about that boy that had me so far gone, but I was about to regret it soon.

"Where you think you going?" He looked down at me with a sinister smirk, which meant he was up to no good. He grabbed me by my neck, making my heart jump and eyes widen as his smile disappeared. His handsome face became distorted and demon-like.

"You ain't going nowhere." He threw my body on the bed and laid on top of me. I could feel his hard-on touching my upper thigh through his sweat pants.

"Rico, please. I don't want to, and I'm on my period," I sobbed as he leaned in, trying to kiss me. I turned my head away, trying to avoid his lips.

That only made him angrier. He grabbed my chin forcefully, almost breaking it, and turned my face towards his, leaning in to kiss me once more. I shut my eyes and silently cried while attempting to tuck my lips in. He snaked his tongue and pried my mouth open.

"Hmmm," he moaned inside my mouth.

I tried moving, but it was no use until I felt him tugging at my shorts.

"No," I said, pushing his hands off me. He drew back and punched me dead in my mouth. Blood poured out rapidly, and I could've sworn I felt my teeth loosen.

I yelped like a wounded dog. As he forced himself inside me and began pumping in and out of me, I laid there in agony, trying to zone out and dream of myself anywhere but there.

I hoped someone would bust in at that moment and save me, but I knew that was far from likely.

"You so wet! Oh, my God," he groaned.

He disgusted me.

I tried moving my arms, but he had them pinned above my head.

"You wet for daddy? I'ma get your ass pregnant. You gon' have my baby. You gon' have it. Oh, fuck!" he screeched, building up his nut.

A couple more pumps, and I felt his sweaty body shake and collapse on top of mine. I felt so embarrassed, worthless, and downright dirty. How could someone that claimed they loved me cause me this much pain?

He got up and pulled up his pants, acting like what he did was consensual. Like I had given him permission to violate my body. If I could have curled up into a ball and died, I would have.

Waking up from my nightmare of that day, I wanted to cry. I mean, it was good that I had gotten away from the sick bastard, but I still hadn't come clean to my family about him. I did tell my mom about shit he used to do to me. I just left out the sexual stuff, because Lord knows what she would have done. That situation happened over six months earlier and was the final straw in our situationship.

I grabbed my cell phone off my pillow. It read 5:37 a.m. It was early, but I had to be to work at nine. I worked at the Boys and Girls Club in Charlestown, and we were taking a couple of kids to The Clougherty Pool on Bunker Hill Ave that day. I got up and prepared to take care of my daily hygiene. I grabbed my Twilight Woods body wash and lotion set, Bioré facewash, and teeth whitening kit and made my way to the bathroom. My towel and washcloth were already in the bathroom, which was in the hallway next to my bedroom.

∞ ∞ ∞

The pool was packed. It seemed like everybody and their momma was there. I ignored the thirsty guys as I walked with my group of kids. My coworker Latavia and I were talking amongst ourselves about our freshman year of college and how hype we were until we were interrupted.

"So we meet again," I heard a raspy baritone voice say.

I looked up and couldn't help but melt. Latavia's constant nudging of my rib cage made me do so. I was ready to pop on her ass. But it was the same guy from the basketball court looking down at me, smiling. I couldn't help the smile that graced my face as I looked over at Tavi, who was smiling from ear to ear and looking between us.

"Hey—"

Oh, damn, I forgot his name.

I guess he must've sensed that I forgot, because he said, "Oh, damn, it's like that, ma? You forgot a nigga's name?" He placed his hands over his heart as if he was truly hurt.

I couldn't help but giggle.

"I'm sorry."

"It's all good, ma. My name is Terrence, but you can call me babe, baby, boo... daddy." He chuckled.

I looked at him and fell in love with his dark eyes. Something about them had me captivated.

"Excuse me?" I questioned with my eyebrow raised as I tried to conceal a grin.

He licked his lips and walked up to me until he was invading my personal space.

"You heard what I said." He gave me a once-over. "You gonna be mine."

I held his stare. "Is that right? Don't you date Red?" I questioned with a little sass in my voice and my hand on my hip.

"Oh, so you do remember a nigga? To answer your question, nah, she a cool bit— female, but that's it. I got my eyes on you," Terrence chortled, giving me a one-sided grin. "Can I have your number so I can get to know you better, beautiful?" he asked, turning his head sideways.

"Depends on if you know my name?" I turned my head to the side, repeating his actions.

"Teyanna," he challenged matter-of-factly. He began to chuckle.

I swear, I began to fall in love with his laugh. I decided to join in with a giggle of my own.

"Ok, well, fine. Lemme see your phone."

He looked hesitant at first as I held my hand out. Once I had his phone, I put my phone number and name in it. After giving it back, I tried to walk off and get back to work, but he held my wrist and put the phone to his ear. My phone started to vibrate inside my tote bag.

"I just had to make sure you gave a nigga the right number and weren't playing games."

We laughed in unison. I shook my head, thinking he was unbelievable.

"Boy, bye, ain't nobody playing games but you. Just don't waste my time," I retorted, smiling from ear to ear. Despite my smile, I was serious.

"How? I told you I wanted you, and that I'm gonna get you," he said with a cocky grin.

"We'll see. Just don't forget to use my number." Once he let my hand go, I went to the poolside to watch the smaller children. It seemed to be a good day.

"I will... I will," Terrence said.

I could feel his eyes on my body before he went back over to where his group of friends or whatever were to grab his things and dap up a few people before leaving.

For the rest of my shift, all I could think about was his fine ass and when he would call or text me for our first outing together. I wasn't going to call it a date just yet.

I sent a group text to Lo, Taj, and Eboni, knowing that I'd be too tired to link up with them when I got off work.

Chapter 6

Terrence

*T*he ringing of my phone was constant, and eventually, I had woken all the way up out my sleep. I glanced down at my screen, which was bright as fuck.

"What now, Brianna?" I asked, annoyed.

"Oh, now, you can answer a bitch's calls?!" her voice boomed through the phone.

Brianna was this bad-ass jawn I met up in Brooklyn while I was cruising the block with my bros, and she was dick riding from day one. She and I had been dealing with each other a little over a year. Everything was copacetic until she became psychotic and started stalking me, going through my phone, and fighting other bitches. We weren't anywhere near official, but it seemed like every female I associated with, she wanted me to cut off to please her.

"I've been busy, ma. You already know what I get into. I can't have my hand glued to my phone every five seconds." I spoke nothing but facts.

Of course, I had time to shoot shorty a quick text here and there, but she was aggy as fuck, and quite frankly, I had no desire to wife her. Why waste both our time? Her head game was elite, her pussy was fire, her body looked good, and her face wasn't bad, so it worked for a good minute because she was a nice piece of arm candy. After a while, though, that ain't enough. The bitch only wanted money, bragging rights, and dick, which I was happy to supply when I wasn't tied up, but she didn't have any desire to better herself, and she had a seed. The fuck a nigga like me look like, raising the next man's kid? I couldn't be no step dad or no shit like that.

"Nigga, you got time to be kee-keeing with other bitches but never got time for me?" She scoffed.

I could tell she was on the verge of tears, but I didn't care. That bitch was barking up the wrong tree. I was still tired and mad as fuck because she had called, killing my sleep, crying and worrying about what the fuck I was doing. I was getting ready to put her silly-ass in line.

"Look here, son, what I do is none of your concern. We already discussed that you ain't my bitch, especially with the type of shit you be on. When you call me, come correct. Unless you calling about throwing it back for a nigga, don't hit my line with no bullshit, giving me a headache."

I hung up. I was about to add her dumb ass to the block list like I did all the other lost hoes that couldn't get with the program.

I wasn't the type of nigga to disrespect females. But, trust me, I wasn't no square-ass nigga that you were gonna talk shit to just to act like everything was all kumbaya afterwards. I cut hoes off with no hesitation. When you fucked up with me, there weren't any second chances.

I adjusted my eyes and looked around, realizing I wasn't in my room. I was in Red's. I didn't think I was that bent, so I didn't understand how I managed to pass out there. Red's shiesty ass probably sucked me into it. She was a little Charli Baltimore-looking chick. She used to be basic until I helped shorty level up by giving her a little piece of change to hold some weight at her crib. Not a lot, though. Even though she was obsessed with a nigga, I still ain't trust her too much. I mean, her pussy was bomb, but she wasn't as bad as the shorty I saw at the pool the other day.

Teyanna was beyond beautiful. I felt the chemistry from the first time I laid eyes on her at the park and hadn't gotten her off my mind since then. I just knew I had to have her. That's why I had to strike up a conversation with her and get her number.

I had never been in a real serious relationship before. I ain't know if I was built for a relationship, but lil mama had me contemplating. Everything about her was dope. I had never been so blunt about any female ever, and I knew she was feeling me too. She didn't put herself out there like every other female, though, and she sure didn't throw herself at me. That made me want her more.

I grabbed my space gray iPhone 7 Plus and shot shorty a text. It was a little after nine in the morning, but it was Saturday, so I hoped she wasn't asleep still.

Me: Goodmorning Beautiful ☺

Her: Who's this? :-/

Me: Your soon to be husband :-*

Her: lol Goodmorning Terrence ☺

I smiled just thinking about how I was 'bout to tie that down.

"Damn, that's all I got to say," I thought out loud to myself. She already knew what was up.

Me: haha Sorry I didn't text you sooner, ma. I was out handling some business. When can I take you out?

Her: it's ok, you tell me when you're available.

Me: Let me surprise you. ;) Tonight around 8?

Her: Okay, see you then. I'll send you my address ☺

Teyanna was bad, I mean it. I had only seen her twice, yet every time I saw her, it seemed like I became even more attracted to her. Her chocolate ass could get it, and the fact that nobody could say they had hit made me want her little ass even more. A nigga still had a few hoes that I still fucked every now and again, but it was just that: 'a fuck.' After we were done, there was no kissing and cuddling. I'd break 'em off with some bread until I was ready to hit it again or pass them along to the team, depending on how good them skins was.

I did my homework on lil mama. It seemed like every nigga I knew wanted a piece of Teyanna, but being the good girl she was, she seemed not to give them niggas the time of day. I was lowkey sweating her. I wanted her in the worst way, and I wasn't just talking sexually. I was thinking about the little date we had later that night, and I wanted to be on my p's and q's. But, first, I had shit to do, like going to get up with my Colombian connect. He wanted me to meet him outside of the Bean in Springfield, Massachusetts. He said it was a little more low-key, and he was willing to compensate the price, so I could get my supply at a lower price for a larger and better quantity.

Chino Ramirez was the new El Chapo, basically. Not only did he supply the east coast, but he supplied parts of the south and west. He even had something in Canada. His name held a lot of weight in the streets. Before my uncle V died and handed the torch down to me, I'd had plenty of meetings with Chino. The nigga kinda looked like Allen Payne. His accent was thick as fuck. He had everything from judges, FBI, DEA, and local pigs on his payroll, just like me. He was Mister Untouchable. Niggas could only dream about having the luxuries he had.

I hit up my cousin, Bernard, also known as Bishop. He took on that name from watching the movie *Juice* too much. He even had the nose piercing and shaved his head bald like Tupac at one point. He was always down to ride for anything. My uncle V trained both of us to take over, but changed his mind soon after. Bishop was a fucking hot head. He did a lot of shit without thinking, which made him the muscle while I was the brain behind the whole operation. My uncle had chosen those roles for us before his untimely demise. Bishop didn't seem to like it at first but soon learned he ain't have a choice; it was either get the money or fall back completely. His ass wasn't finna shake me, though.

I sat up in bed, pushing Red's thirsty-ass off me, and waited for him to answer, growing pissed as the phone continued to ring. He knew how important the meeting was.

Once he answered, he sounded all out of breath. From the sound of it, he was probably pounding a bitch's insides.

"Yo," he panted.

I couldn't help but laugh. "Yo, my nigga, be ready in a half-hour to forty-five minutes. We 'bout to go to Springfield," I stated while Red huffed and acted like a big-ass baby.

"Where?" he asked in confusion. "Get the fuck outta here. Can't you see I'm on the phone?" he yelled.

"Nigga, just be ready. It's 'bout to be a white Christmas," I spoke in code, letting him know there would be a shitload of heroin and cocaine for low-ass prices.

"Alright, my dude. I'm 'bout to eat some collard greens with hot sauce," he joked, talking in code about some fire-ass weed.

I laughed, still feeling the effects of last night's alcohol on my breath.

"Yeah, but I'm 'bout to get ready so hurry that shit up," I said, looking at Red trying to get my attention by unveiling her naked body. My dick began to grow a mind of its own.

"A'ight, blood," he said.

I could hear him pulling on the blunt and choking a little.

"One." I ended the call and got ready to make some moves. Just as I hung up, Red straddled my lap. She had just returned from the bathroom. My guess was from brushing her teeth; she knew I hated morning breath.

"Daddy," she said with a saddened look.

I knew her ass was about to start begging.

"Wassup," I said, holding her hips. My soldier was standing at attention. I needed to be in something tight, wet, and warm. Red was the most convenient at the moment, so I was gon' play along with her little game.

"I need some money so I can pay my rent." She began to kiss my neck.

"I just gave you money for your rent and then some," I responded, letting go of her waist and looking her dead in her grill, daring her to lie. Her little neck kisses weren't doing the trick, but I knew what would, though. I saw Red's little sister, Daja, enter the room with no clothes on. They were roommates and lived together off my dime, but, as that saying goes, nothing in this world is free.

"Good morning, daddy," Daja said as Red removed herself from my lap. Even though Red was bad as a muthafucka, Daja was badder, but she was a hoodrat. Her ass stayed in every nigga's face. There were niggas who had videos of themselves running trains on her. Bitch was a lost soul, and I wasn't tryna save nobody. I had to give props to shorty, though. She was about her money. She made sure she got paid for everything she did. She ain't care about what niggas and bitches had to say.

"So what y'all tryna do for some bread?" I challenged boldly.

Daja reached forward and grabbed my rod that was already peeking through my boxers. Red then grabbed Daja's face by her chin. They kissed passionately, like they weren't sisters or some shit. Red wrapped her hands around my dick as well, and they both stroked my shit.

Once they broke the kiss, they began taking turns wildin' on my shit like they were in some sort of competition. Red decided to one up her sis, who had just massaged and licked my balls. Red began to do some nasty shit as she spit on my dick before taking most of me into her mouth with no hands.

"Damn," I said, throwing my head back and pumping into her face. I honestly ain't care which freak hoe swallowed my nut. I just knew I needed to bust one so I could bounce. After a couple more minutes of Daja massaging and slurping my balls while Red sucked my dick, I was close to bussing. I had to close my eyes and bite the inside of my lip to keep from calling out like a little bitch.

Before I knew it, I was shooting my babies in Red's mouth, and she ain't pull away until I was all done. Then, what she did next had me watching in awe.

She faced Daja, who was waiting with her mouth open like a bird receiving food from its mother. I didn't think I had ever met any bitches as freaky as them.

After I got dressed, I dropped a huge stack on the bed and got up outta there before I fucked around and ended up extremely late to the meeting.

Instead of getting to Springfield in an hour and a half like the directions had told me, it took me almost three, thanks to all the fucked-up traffic. Springfield reminded me of a dirtier version of the Bronx. A few of my niggas from the city had moved up there because it was better for them business-wise. I ain't really know how true that statement was.

"Yo, what street this nigga say he was on again?" Bishop questioned, looking around.

"Alwin or Alvin some shit like that," I said, passing a sign that said: "Welcome to Sixteen Acres."

"Nigga said his prices and everything were better. He got this whole shit on lockdown," I explained to Bishop. I had already had my info on Chino. Bishop ain't care about all that. All he needed to hear was 'more money,' and I had his vote.

Pulling up to the house, Bishop and I made sure we were strapped and aware of our surroundings. Bishop gave me a head nod, signaling that he was down for whatever. We had two carloads of our most trusted hittas from Boston just in case shit went left.

Walking through the house, a nigga scanned around and was impressed. The neighborhood was alright, but the house was dope and reminded me of a spot on MTV Cribs. That nigga, Chino, was short, standing at five foot seven, but I could feel his presence. It spoke volumes. He had olive-colored skin and jet-black hair, which he had slicked back with a part on the side. He was dressed in a tailor-made suit and didn't seem like the flashy type at all. Matter fact, he kept shit simple but still looked like money.

He was the first to speak. *"Mi chico,* Terror. *¿Cómo estás?"* he asked, shaking my hand. He turned to Bishop. "Bishop, I have only heard good things about you."

"I'm good. And you?" I responded as Chino sat behind his cherry wood desk and offered us a seat. He pulled out a thick Cuban cigar and lit it before offering Bishop and me one.

I respectfully declined, but Bishop took it, and they began puffing together.

"Let's get down to business, shall we? I usually sell for twenty-five, but I like you, Terror and Bishop. I like you guys a lot. You remind me of me and my brother. God, rest his soul," he said. He looked saddened by the mention of his brother but quickly regained his composure and cleared his throat.

"I'll give it to y'all for seventeen for coke and twenty for heroin. I trust that you guys will be ready to receive the first shipment in three days." He stood up with his hand out, waiting to seal the deal.

I looked at Bishop. It was like we'd hit the jackpot. We both stayed calm while shaking his hand. Shit was looking up for us young niggas.

We agreed that I would handle everything with our Jamaican connect before switching all the way over and also planned to add more security just in case shit got messy.

Chapter 7

Lauryn

"That's why I need you to go to The Galleria with me," Tey begged while standing in my room. That hoe ain't even call firs. She just came and woke me up out my sleep and shit. She lucky I loved her ass, 'cause if it had been any other person, they would've surely caught an earful and probably these hands.

She was going on a date that night with the fine-ass nigga we saw at the basketball court about a week earlier. She saw him the day before while she was at work, and he had already asked her on a date. I was happy my main bitch was moving on from that sucka-ass nigga, Rico. Plus, Terror was mouthwatering and paid. I heard he was the plug.

I finally gave in. "Okay, fine, thot," I laughed, sliding out of bed.

"Yesssss!" she said, smiling hard while hopping up and down and clapping her hands like a big-ass kid.

"Where he taking you?" I asked, dragging my feet and looking in my closet for something to wear. I finally decided on some light, stonewashed, high-waisted, ripped jean shorts with a white, off-shoulder crop top, and some wolf-grey 11s.

"I don't know. He ain't say yet. He wants to surprise me," she replied while texting. She was laid out on my bed, cheesing from ear to ear.

I knew it was him. "What he say?" I asked, wanting to be nosey.

"None of your business, nosey," she said, chuckling.

Before I could respond with one of my smart remarks, her phone starting ringing. She looked nervous as hell and almost hesitant to pick up. Mentally calming herself down and inhaling, she got ready.

"Hello," she said, cheesing and showing all thirty-two teeth.

I mouthed for her to put it on speaker, and she was reluctant to do so, but she agreed.

"Hey, beautiful," he said. She couldn't help but to chortle while listening to him.

"Hi, handsome," she giggled.

She was up, walking around and talking to him. She couldn't sit still. I remembered that feeling.

"How you sleep, ma?" he asked sincerely.

It kind of made me jealous because it reminded me of how Nas used to talk to me at the beginning of our relationship, but after five years and with him being all the way in North Carolina playing basketball, I was lucky if I got a text from him every couple of days.

"I slept good. How about you, hun?"

I playfully rolled my eyes and bit down hard to keep from laughing. She grabbed one of my pillows and threw it at me, but I moved my head in the nick of time. I continued looking down at my phone and saw that I had a text from my one and only, Nasir Lavell Huddleston. He hadn't called or texted me in almost two weeks, but it was just like him to hit me up whenever he wanted while I texted and called him, only to be ignored.

Him: Babeeeeeee <3.<3

Him: I miss you

Me: Hi Nas :-/

I guess he didn't like my response, 'cause, less than a minute later, he called my phone. I walked out the room. Once in the living room, I answered.

"What, Nasir?" I rolled my eyes, sucking my teeth.

"Nasir? I ain't 'daddy' no more? Like, wassup with your attitude?"

I had to look at the phone and blow out a frustrated breath.

"You ain't shit!" I stated through gritted teeth. "Now you got time to hit me up for the first time in what? Two weeks? And you think we still together? You dumber than you sound."

"Listen! Just hear me out. I've been busy. Coach been riding our asses. We lost two games in a row, and he not easing up on us. Lo, I promise I ain't worried about these thots. I've been busy, bae. I swear there ain't nobody but you."

I rolled my eyes. That story was starting to get played out. Usually, I went right along with that shit and sucked in every word he said like a fucking sponge, but not that time. I was tired of him putting everything and everyone before me. I needed to put myself first.

"Whatever, Nas. Save it 'cause, quite frankly, I don't care for your excuses anymore. You're always too busy for me, so let's just dead this shit right now. It's a waste of both our time." It pained my heart as those words left my mouth, but it didn't feel the same anymore. It felt like I was putting my all into it when didn't give two shits whether our relationship worked or not.

"You're not going nowhere. I'm not letting you go, Lo. We been in this shit for far too long for me to give up that easy and let you go. I just can't."

As he spoke, I felt tears building up at the rim of my eyes and threatening to fall down my face. Whenever I wanted out of the relationship, he wanted to pour his heart out and talk all that sweet shit. I slowly felt myself getting sucked back in.

"Look, Nas, just lemme think about it, okay? This long distance is killing me, baby. I'm not used to this," I said, crying silently.

I blew out my breath in frustration.

"Baby, listen, you know I love you, and I'm only here to make a better life for the both of us. I'm gonna make sure our future is good. I'm gonna marry you one day. Word to my mother, I am. I just need you to ride out for me."

When he mentioned marrying me, I couldn't help but have those words repeat in my mind, causing me to grin hard as I wiped my eyes and sniffled, nodding my head as if he was right in front of me.

"For real?" I asked, feeling all happy and giddy all over again.

"Yeah, we soulmates, remember?" he teased.

'Soulmates' was some corny shit we made up when we were younger. We ain't know shit about that word.

We laughed.

"Yes," I said as I heard Tey come out the room, yelling my name. "Look, baby, I gotta go. Can you FaceTime me tonight?"

"Of course, wifey," he said. "But I'm 'bout to go out real quick with the team; I'll text you in the meantime."

"Okay, well, I'm 'bout to go out with Tey. Love you," I said, holding up one finger to Tey, letting her know I was almost done.

"I love you too, sexy. Tell my little god sis I said 'whaddup?' I'ma text her ass later." He ended the call.

"Alright, I'm ready," I said, placing my phone in my back pocket.

"Who was that?" Tey questioned as she walked toward the front door.

"Guh, who else? Your godbrother's monkey ass said 'whaddup?' and he's gonna text you later,'" I said as we walked out the front door and to her car.

"Awww," she cooed. "I miss him." She unlocked the doors and slid into the driver's seat.

"Me too, sis," I said.

∞ ∞ ∞

One hour later

"Bitch, we been in this mall for almost thirty minutes, and you ain't find shit you like yet?" I asked, getting annoyed.

Tey's picky ass could never make up her damn mind, but her fits looked like she stepped fresh off a runway when she popped out.

"Shut up!" she said, looking through the racks at the Guess store. She held up the all-black Deena flocked-lace bodysuit.

"Uh-Oh!" I yelled. "My bitch tryna be on her grown and sexy shit tonight."

She went to another rack and pulled out a black, high-waisted bandage skirt.

"Hell yeah. I'm gonna try and wear some heels." She tilted her head to the side, sticking out her tongue. "What you think?" she asked, giving me a look that read 'bitch, you better validate me.'

"Yesssss, bitch, he finna be on you!"

"Ayeeee!" She did a little twerk as the white people looked at us like we were crazy, but we ain't give a damn.

We walked up to the counter and the nice, older, blonde white lady rung us up while making small talk.

"Okay, that'll be one hundred sixty-nine dollars and seventy-two cents, please," she said while folding the stuff neatly and putting it into a bag.

Tey pulled out two fresh Benjis, handed them to the cashier, and turned toward me.

"I can't wait for tonight," she gushed for about the hundredth time today.

"Yeah, I know, hoe. You told me a million times. Just don't give it up," I joked.

"Receipt in the bag, okay, ma'am?" the cashier asked Tey, who nodded.

Tey grabbed the bag and the change, and we made our way to the food court. We decided on Panda Express. Once she and I picked out what we wanted, we sat at a table and made small talk. In the midst of us talking about how she was going to do her hair and makeup, she froze, and her eyes became fixated on something behind her.

"Bitch, what's wrong?"

My eyes followed hers, and they damn near bulged out of my head when I saw a very angry Rico, with a few of his niggas in tow, walking over to our table. I knew it was about to be some shit, but I had my girl's back.

"So this is the only way I can talk to your dumb ass. You can't answer my calls or text a nigga back, like you busy or some shit." He had the nerve to be standing over my home girl, grilling her.

I honestly hated the ground that nigga walked on, and he always tried to pretend like he was a good dude, but it turned out my judgment was right. He wasn't shit at all.

She seemed so embarrassed as people looked at us. I could tell she was frightened to speak up for herself, so I took the initiative to do so.

"Uh-uh, we not doing this. Come on, Tey, let's go," I said, grabbing her hand and standing up until he pushed her shoulder back down, forcing her to sit.

"Nah, you can go. She ain't going nowhere." Rico waved me off like I was bothering him. I looked at the nigga like he was dumb.

"She's not your fucking child, my nigga. Move so we can leave. You're wasting our time, she don't want you."

Shocked, his boys looked at him, wondering what he was gonna do next.

"Rico, please just move. I don't wanna talk to you. I just wanna go," Teyanna said as she began to get frustrated.

I knew she wanted to cry because, no matter how many times she tried to get away from him, he always seemed to be lurking in the shadows, waiting to come out and stake his claim on what he thought belonged to him.

"Oh, word?" he said, looking at her quizzingly and daring her to agree.

"Yes," she said, her voice barely above a whisper.

"Alright, fuck you and this dumb bitch," he said, referring to me as he knocked our food off the table.

I had to bite the inside of my lip to contain myself.

"Eboni take care of me real well, anyways. I'm thinking about knocking her ass up again," he boasted as he turned to his niggas and slapped hands with a few of 'em as they laughed.

Teyanna's neck snapped towards him. I looked at her for a response. She looked confused, hurt, and angry, and then her face turned into a stonewall.

"Oh, word, Frederick? That's how we doing shit now?" she questioned. Her fists were clenched.

"That's what I been doing for a minute now," he said with a devilish grin.

I walked over to Tey and hooked my arm with hers.

"Let's go, Tey. Don't let this no-good-ass nigga get to you. You can do better, sis," I said. We didn't need to hear anymore. That meant our speculations were right all along.

"Well, I hope it was good, Rico. Have a nice life. I'm done with you. Next time you think about killing yourself, call her," she said with a smile before grabbing her bag and sashaying away before security walked over. Rico was now spazzing out, trying to chase her down, and flipping shit in the food court.

Minutes later, we were back in Teyanna's car.

"I'ma murk that bitch!" Teyanna said, her eyes focused on the road as she sped through the streets of Boston.

"That bitch done fucked up. I told you that bitch was grimy," I agreed, adding in my own two cents, 'cause I was heated too. Eboni had the nerve to smile and be buddy-buddy with us when she knew she was being a low-down slut bucket. I was ready to put hands and feet on her.

"I knowww," she said. I heard her choking on her words.

"She was fucking that nigga while he was with me, then had the balls to sit and smile in my face?" she asked more to herself than to me, as if she was putting the pieces together. She gripped the steering wheel tighter and began to cry.

I rubbed her back. I wanted to cry with her, but I didn't wanna get in a damn car accident.

"Listen, pull over, T. Let me drive. I can drive us to my house."

She wiped her face and began to huff and puff.

"We ain't going to your house. We going to see this bitch first, and I want her to lie to my face so I can fuck her up even more than I'm about to," she snarled angrily.

I sat back 'cause I knew Teyanna's hands were lethal, especially when someone forced her hand, and this was something that was long overdue. I wasn't the type to jump bitches, but I wanted to throw in a few hits of my own.

Chapter 8

Eboni

I t had been a couple days since I last talked to Rico, and I had been in a mild depressed phase. Why couldn't he just love me and be all about me the same way I was all about him? I loved him with all my heart, and he continually treated me like shit.

My phone started ringing, taking me out of my thoughts. It was Teyanna for the tenth time that day. That bitch was the last person I wanted to talk to. She was the reason I was going through most of that shit with Rico.

I pressed decline and placed her on the block list because I knew she was just gonna keep calling. Best friend or not, I wanted Rico; he was mine. I decided to do something to get my mind off the whole Rico situation. I started to undress so I could take a nice hot bath and try to relax with some candles since I was home alone.

Two hours later

I got lost in my thoughts, but I finally got out the tub, went into the living room, and began watching *The First 48*. Before I knew it, I had dozed off, but that didn't last long.

Bang, bang, bang.

I jumped off the couch and made my way to the front door to see who it was. As I peeked through the peephole, I saw that it was Teyanna.

"What the fuck?" I swung open the door with an attitude that could be felt across the city. "Why you do that, T? I was s—"

I didn't get to complete my sentence before her fist came forward and punched me in my mouth. She followed up by punching me in my eye before I could react. I instantly felt my eye swell shut as she continued raining blows all over my face and body. I tried to fight back, but that made her angrier, and she proceeded to grab my little bit of hair and pull me to the ground.

"Get that thot-ass bitch!" Lo cheered.

"You dirty, conniving bitch! You a fraud-ass hoe! How could you do this to me?!"

As Teyanna kicked me in my head and stomach, I felt like I was gonna pass the fuck out.

"T, calm down. You're gonna kill the bitch," Lauryn intervened. A few moments later, I felt Teyanna's body being lifted off of me.

At that moment, I was so grateful. Then, I heard her walk over to me and lean down next to my ear.

"You can thank Rico," she said, standing up straight and hawking up as much spit as she could before spitting in my hair and face. She then kicked me in my stomach one last time before walking away as I lay moaning and groaning on the hallway floor until an old Puerto Rican lady came out screaming for help. I felt my eyes getting heavier as a liquid gushed from between my legs. I reached my hand down in fear. When I saw my hand, panic set in.

It was blood. A lot of it. I began to cramp bad, and I felt like I was about to die. Before I could say anything, everything went blank.

When I woke up, I saw my mother in the corner, weeping with my brothers, who hugged her. My little sister was sitting in the hospital chair at the foot of my bed.

"Mom... she's up?" My sister, Kiana, perked up a little, and my mom's eyes darted over to me while she raced over to my bedside.

"Thank God," she cried out, lifting her hands towards the ceiling and clasping them in a prayer-like motion as she hovered over my weak body and placed kisses on my face.

"Kiana, go get the nurse and let them know she's up. Boys, go to the vending machine while I talk to your sister," my mom directed while handing the boys money.

Once they dispersed out of the room, my mom grabbed a nearby chair and sat near my bed.

"What happened?" she asked.

I pondered on whether I wanted to let her know the truth, that my best friend had beaten my ass for betraying her in the worst way, or if I wanted to hide the truth and seek my own revenge.

"I don't remember, Mom," I said as I turned my head away to avoid eye contact.

"You're lying, Eboni. I can tell," she said as she gently grabbed my face and turned it to her.

"Mom, I really don't wanna talk about it right now," I snatched my face away.

My mom was in the middle of saying something when Kiana and the nurse entered.

The first words the nurse uttered were, "Hi, Eboni. I'm Sylvia, and I'm one of the nurses here at Boston Medical."

"Hey," I said dryly.

"You lost a lot of blood, Ms. Walker. We were able to save your life, but your baby, on the other hand, did not make it."

"Baby?!" me and my mother said in unison. I could feel my mom's eyes burning a hole on the side of my face. I was scared to look at her.

"Yes, ma'am. The fetus seemed to be anywhere between six to eight weeks. I'm so sorry," she said, looking between me and my mom. She continued telling me about the other injuries and broken bones, but I didn't care about any of that. I had just lost a fucking child I ain't even know I was having.

How could I be that far along and not even know? That was me and Rico's child, and that bitch had the nerve to kill it. I wanted her blood so bad I could taste it.

After that, I didn't feel like being bothered anymore. You know the Jakes had to come questioning me about if I knew anyone who wanted to harm me, and did I feel like I was still in danger. They eventually left after me telling them the same shit I told my mother. I didn't know and I didn't remember. Once everyone was gone, I cried by myself, upset that I'd put myself in that position. I had to stay in the hospital an extra day so that they could monitor me. I was devastated. It wasn't fair. My child ain't deserve that.

Shortly after I pulled myself together, there was a knock on the door, and Rico waltzed in without a care in the world, looking as good as ever. Boy, did I wish he could feel like I was feeling. I blew his phone up almost thirty times and left a dozen messages telling him to meet me at the hospital and that it was an emergency. Suddenly, there he was, and I was at a loss for words.

"What the fuck happened, yo?" he asked, sounding concerned and looking confused.

"What did you tell that bitch?" I sassed, sitting up with my arms folded.

"What bitch, bruh?"

"Teyanna, nigga!" I yelled. I wasn't worried about my roommate hearing me because they had taken her out for some x-rays.

"I ain't tell her ass shit, mane," he said as he looked at me, annoyed and kind of offended that I would insinuate something like that. I knew he was lying, though. The nigga could barely look me in my eyes, which let me know something was up.

"She beat my ass, talking some bullshit about me being a fucked up friend, and I'm supposed to believe you ain't say shit?!" I started to bawl my eyes out.

"Cut that crying shit out, mane! I ain't told her ass shit! I haven't even talked to her stupid ass, yo!"

I wasn't buying that shit, so I decided to tell him just what the fuck he did.

"Well, her and that bitch, Lauryn, decided to pull up to my house for whatever reason and jump me. I swear to God, this is all your fucking fault!" I lied as he began pacing the room at the foot of my bed. I could tell his wheels were turning in his head while he processed everything that was going on.

"And I lost our baby!" I said, causing him stop in his tracks like a deer caught in headlights. He gave me a glare like he wanted to kill my ass. For a second, I wanted to press the emergency call button.

He finally spoke up after what felt like forever.

"Fuck did you just say?" His voice boomed so loud, I was scared as fuck to repeat myself.

I bit on my bottom lip, drawing a little bit of blood. I was damn near jumping out of my skin. I knew it was a bad-ass idea to enter a situation with that crazy-ass nigga, but I couldn't help myself. I was attracted to his thuggish demeanor initially. Now, I was in physical and mental pain because of a nigga that didn't even love me the way I loved him. What the fuck had I gotten myself into?

"I said..." I swallowed hard before continuing. "I lost our baby, Rico, when Teyanna and Lauryn jumped me."

"Our baby?" He glared at me, and I couldn't tell what his emotions were. It was as if he was masking them or something.

I sat cautiously while keeping the remote with the call button close by.

"Yes," I muttered.

"Did you tell Tey?" He gulped, running his hands through his scruffy hair. I had to look up and look at that nigga like he was the dumbest muthafucka I'd ever met.

What wasn't that nigga getting? She ain't want him and I did.

"You more worried about that bitch finding out about our fucking baby than you are about her killing our child?!" I yelled out, frustrated. Like, I was getting my ass beat and some more shit over this retarded-ass nigga. Not to mention, I ruined an almost ten-year friendship, and he was worried about the sadity bitch finding out when she didn't even want him.

"Don't call her a bitch no more," he warned.

My heart felt like it had been shattered, ripped out, ran over, and stabbed a thousand times.

"What?! You know what, fuck you and that bitch. As soon as I get out of here, I'm pressing charges, but not before I tell her about our creation," I said while giving him an evil grin.

That smile soon faded because, before I knew it, Rico had his hand wrapped tightly around my neck. I didn't even have enough time to press the call button.

"Listen here, you dumb bitch. Try that shit if you want to, and I'll body your dumb ass. Word to my mother," he said. He had a death glare in his eyes as he grinded his teeth.

How the fuck was I scared in the hospital? This nigga was crazy just like Teyanna told me, and it was too late to realize it and step away. I was in too deep.

"I'm... sorry," I struggled to say as he applied more and more pressure. I could hear the machines I was hooked up to making weird noises. Soon after, I began to feel lightheaded.

I thought Rico was gonna try and kill me, but he finally let go and threw my head into the pillow as I grabbed my neck, tears staining my cheeks as I selfishly sucked in as much air as possible.

"You just got me vexed. I'm out of here. Make sure you keep your fucking dick suckers shut. I'll hit you up when you stop acting stupid," he said before walking out the door.

Chapter 9

Taj

"So what happened again?" I said before pulling on the blunt three times and passing it to Teyanna, who still seemed too upset to explain the story. I turned and listened to Lauryn, who gave me the whole rundown blow by blow.

To say I was shocked would have been an understatement. I never expected 'the bro', Ebz, to be so grimy, but everything started to click.

"The bitch was fucking Rico's dusty ass on the low!" Lo's loud, animated ass started moving and hopping around. I couldn't help but laugh, but the situation was nowhere near funny.

I looked over at Teyanna. She was just puffing on the blunt and staring into outer space. Teyanna barely smoked or drank; she was more of the designated driver, so I knew she must've been going through it.

"Damn, Tey, I'm sorry," I whispered, feeling the need to comfort my sis as I sat on the staircase next to her and pulled her into a hug.

"I'm good." Her voice broke.

"No, you're not, and that's okay." I lifted her chin and looked her deep in her eyes. My sister was hurting bad, and I needed to be there for her. I swear to God, I probably would've slapped Eboni's thot ass up a few times my damn self. How she let dick come between our sisterhood?

"Damn, bitch, can I smoke, too?" Lo half-joked, trying to lighten the mood, but Tey was so high and spaced out that she didn't hear her.

I decided to just roll another blunt.

Teyanna finally spoke. "Damn, that bitch really did that shit! To me, though? Out of all fucking people, she did this to me! That bitch is low, and I'm not done with her yet; she better pray," Tey hissed as Lauryn and I stared at her like she was crazy, 'cause the bitch had been silent since they arrived. I knew she was thirty-eight hot, but she needed to pipe down.

"Um, sissy, you ok, boo?" I asked, but all she did was shrug and look at me with saddened eyes, so I continued. "I know shit got you fucked up, but you ain't gonna go to jail or die over this bitch! I know how you feel, and you know that. It's not worth it, and I'm not gonna let you do it."

She stared at me for a minute, processing the facts I'd just spit her way. Then, she perked up a little bit and slightly grinned.

"Oh, you right, I ain't gon' die. If anything, I'd take that cum guzzler with me."

Me and Lo to burst into laughter. Sis was really off her rocker, but we let her rant.

"I ain't want that nigga, anyways, with his broke ass, plus I got Terrence's fine ass on my back!" She flipped her hair as we all laughed.

"Yeah, bitch, and y'all supposed to link tonight. You better go home and get ready," Lauryn reminded her.

"Hold the fuck up. Tonight?" I held my hand up while looking back and forth between the two of them.

"Yes, bitch, yes," Lo sang as she took another pull on the blunt while dancing. I shook my head, laughing at her silliness.

"Oh my God. What fucking time is it?!" Teyanna hopped up, screaming like her ass was on fire, kind of scaring my ass. She looked at her phone, and she only had two hours to go home and get ready.

"Alright, y'all, I gotta go!" she said, rushing off the stoop and almost twisting her ankle. Shit had both me and Lo in tears 'cause we had never seen her that happy about a date, considering the fact that Rico was her first and only boyfriend.

All I knew was that Terror needed to treat my sister right because I had no problem laying hands on his ass.

Me and Lo went into her house as soon as Teyanna pulled off. We began to have our own little conversation.

"That nigga a snake; I been telling her that. I been warned her about that thot-ass bitch, too, but she ain't wanna listen. Tey is too nice to these hoes," Lo said, sitting on the bed.

"You right, my nigga, but I'm glad she knows wassup now and washed that hoe," I said, laughing and dapping up Lo. Teyanna was our sister. Of course, we fucked with Eboni once upon a time, but she started moving funny and became a thot. Then, rumors started circulating that she was spreading our business. After a while, we kind of distanced ourselves from her, but she ain't get the hint we ain't fuck with her like that. She stayed around, constantly wanting to chill with us and be all up in our business, which we didn't share.

"What's been up with you and my nigga Nas?" I played with her TV remote until I landed on the latest episode of *Scandal* while sitting on the futon in her room.

"I don't know, Taj. We just ain't seeing eye to eye right now. I'm thinking about just hanging that whole shit up," she said.

I gave her the side eye; she looked so stressed out, and I could tell she was torn.

To me, Lo and Nas seemed like the perfect couple, but since we graduated high school and he moved to the south for college, it seemed like they were struggling to keep their relationship afloat.

"It'll be okay, boo. He loves you, and you love him. Shit may seem difficult as fuck, but if you guys communicate and trust each other, it'll go smoother." I glanced back at the TV.

"Yeah, you right, sis. I just don't know what to do," she said, laying on her bed and playing with her phone. A few minutes later, she was laughing and blushing.

"Girl, if you don't shut up," I joked.

"You shut up. I'm talking to my hubby. Hold on, I'm going to the bathroom real quick." She beamed, hopping up with her phone in her hand.

"With your phone?" I grinned with a raised eyebrow.

"Mind your business," she giggled while opening her door and walking out into the hall on her way to the bathroom.

"NASTYYY!" I called out after her while doubled over in laughter.

Chapter 10

Terrence

"Hey, ma, I'm outside," I announced into the phone. I hung up. Sitting on the hood of my diamond-white, metallic 2018 Mercedes-Benz E63 AMG, I had on a Burberry crew neck with my black-and-white NY fitted cap, black Balmain jeans, and black-and-white Balenciaga sneakers. Not to mention, I was wearing about six chains. I had just copped some new round cut twenty-four-carat earrings and a big-faced Rollie from Cartier. Yeah, a nigga was stunting hard. As soon as the door swung open, my mouth dropped, and I couldn't help but adjust my dick on the sly.

Teyanna emerged, and she was looking good as fuck. I could imagine doing everything possible to her fine ass. Her naturally long hair was slicked up into a nice, neat bun. She was rocking a black dress that hugged her curves perfectly, and she had on some nice sandals that showed off her perfectly manicured feet. I could tell she had on makeup, but it wasn't too heavy. She was breathtaking, and I was ready to skip dinner and have her ass for dessert. I had to play it cool, though. I wasn't no thirsty-ass dude.

"Damn, ma, you look gorgeous." I got off the car and made my way toward her. I grabbed her hand and pulled it up, watching her twirl in a circle as I caught a whiff of Chanel perfume. Once again, a nigga wanted to fuck her.

I leaned down, pulling her into my embrace. I had to control myself and be a gentleman. I gave her a light peck on the cheek.

"Thank you. You look handsome." She couldn't stop smiling, and that shit was contagious.

I walked over to the passenger's side of my car and opened the door for her.

"This is your car?" she looked at me in shock.

I couldn't help but nod my head up and down boastfully.

"Where is Terrence? Let him go."

I sat on the bed. What the fuck was going on?

"Rico, don't do it. Put the gun down."

I felt her body jump as her eyes opened. They were filled with tears.

She saw me and broke down in my arms, causing me to hold on to her for dear life.

"Baby, what's wrong?" I asked.

She sobbed harder. "He...he...he..."

"It's okay. Calm down, ma. I need you to talk to me." Massaging her back and rubbing her scalp, I placed light kisses on her forehead.

I rocked her in my arms until I heard her sniffling.

"What's wrong, ma? What was that dream about?"

She explained to me that Rico was her ex-boyfriend and the dumb-ass nigga had been popping up at her crib, stalking her in public, and even putting a gun to her head. In the beginning, before me and shorty started kicking it, I did my research on the nigga and found out he sold a little bit of weight. I found out where the nigga lived, who his mom and brother were, and who his pops was, which I wasn't sure Tey knew, because, if she did, she probably would have been sick.

I was on fire. I felt like I should've done more to protect her, but I wouldn't let my face show it. I ain't feel threatened at all by that bottom-feeder. He was off his rocker. I was gon' see that nigga as soon as I touched back down in Beantown. For the time being, I had to let my princess know I was a man and I was gon' handle it and protect her no matter what.

"That nigga the least of my worries. I'ma handle that when we get back," I vowed.

"Please don't do anything crazy. I don't wanna lose you," she said, looking saddened by the thought.

Looking at her, a nigga felt like using the L-word. I mean, what wasn't to love?

"I can't promise that I won't do anything crazy, but I promise I'ma make it back to you. Get up. Your girls here," I said, trying to lighten the mood as I stood and walked toward the closet to pick out something good to wear for the day.

She quickly wiped her eyes and started cheesing. "Oh my God! How did they get here?" she shrieked as she stood up on the bed and jumped up and down.

"Girl, your ass better stop jumping on my bed." I hungrily watched her breasts bounce. My monster was starting to wake up.

"Yeah, whatever." She plopped down on the bed.

"You want a spanking?" I grinned while walking over to my dresser and pulling out my colorful Coogi sweater with the matching hat.

"No, papi," she replied with her fake Spanish accent.

"Then, get up and get dressed. We going to Ma Dukes' house for dinner tonight after I come home from handling something," I said as I prepared to drag her to the shower with me before we separated.

Chapter 19

Eboni

J had finally mustered up enough courage to go out and live a little. Only form of communication I had with others over the past couple weeks was via social media or text. Nobody was really checking for me besides a couple nosey muthafuckas who wanted to know what happened between me and Teyanna. Not even Rico's sorry ass hit me up like that anymore, but it was cool, though. I was sure he'd seen that she'd been all over social media, flaunting her new nigga.

It was okay 'cause that shit wasn't gon' last. I had plans to shatter that happy fairytale bullshit she was living in. I was gon' fuck up her whole world in the blink of an eye. I called the one person I was sure could make that happen.

"Hello," she answered.

"Wassup, bitch? You ready to do that for me?" I questioned, getting right down to it.

"Yeah, sure. What you needed me to do again?"

"I need you to claim your man back so I can fuck up this bitch, Teyanna's, life." I rolled my eyes while looking around my dirty-ass room. There really hadn't been a need to clean since Rico hadn't been coming over.

"Bitch never had my man. I can tell you that! He just having fun, but Terror knows where home is. He need a rider, not some little-ass girl," she stated. I could sense anger in her voice, but she tried to play it off with a laugh.

"Mhmm, I know that's right. Anyways, make sure you hold up your end of the bargain, Red."

The bitch was ugly as fuck to me. I didn't know why a man of Terrence's stature had any dealings with that peasant. I mean, she had the body, and she was a light-skinned, high-yellow bitch that dyed her hair and eyebrows red, but the bitch and her personality were loud. She was a hood rat from Mattapan with no real home training, yet the bitch was steady pulling niggas that had money. Maybe it was because of the tons of makeup she wore. She was chopped and screwed.

"I got you. You seem a little obsessed with this girl though, boo. Ain't you the one that stole her man?" she asked. I knew she was pissed 'cause I threw shade at her, but she ain't have to throw the whole damn tree at me.

"No, he's been mine just like Terror been yours. Anyways, my nigga, meet me at Chez Vous tomorrow night at nine." I wanted Teyanna's head, but I had to devise part two of my plan first, which was to steal her man.

"Okay, then. See ya." She hung up.

I laughed at my own devious thoughts, which were soon interrupted by a constant pounding at the front door. I groaned in agony because I was the only one home. My mom was out with her so-called best friend, and my siblings were at school.

"Who is it?" I asked.

"It's me, Eb. Open up, damn. It's cold." I heard that annoying-ass black ant yell from the other side of the door as I unlocked the three locks.

There stood my mother's bum-ass husband, who had been M.I.A. for days. The nigga smelled like something had died. His eyes were wide open and glassy. I could tell he was high and probably on the move to find something else to sell. I held my hand up to my nose as I watched him waltz into the house and disappear into the room him and my mother shared.

I quickly went to my room and closed my door while lying in bed. As soon as I turned on my phone to scroll down my Facebook newsfeed, Harry burst into my room like a madman.

"What the fuck?!" I shouted as he stumbled his funky ass into my room uninvited.

"Eb, lemme hold five dollars. I promise I'll give it back later," he said, his eyes moving around my room.

"I don't have no money, Harry, sorry," I said, dismissing him.

"Yeah, you do. Look at all that shit you got. You mean to tell me your dad ain't send you no money this week?"

"Nah," I stated. I didn't trust that nigga. That was why I had a knife stuffed underneath my pillow. Not because he had touched me recently, but because the nightmares hadn't stopped. I constantly stayed on my toes, and that knife was about to come in handy.

"Whatever, you dumb bitch, you think you better than me?" he asked, getting visibly upset while I just huffed and cleared my throat while scrolling through my phone.

"Goodbye, Harry." In my mind, nobody understood what it was like to have a sicko for a stepfather. My mother was so far up that nigga's ass that whatever he did, she was fine with. When he sold all the jewelry and our flat screen and stole all our

Christmas presents to feed his own selfish addiction, she took him back. I never told her the deepest secret of them all, though: that he loved and touched her innocent baby girl, Eboni, when she wasn't around. It had been over five years, but I never felt safe when I was alone with him.

I didn't mask the hate that I had for him while I was around my mother. She would always say I was a child and needed to stay in a child's place or leave. I was trying, but her husband didn't seem to grasp that. He stole my innocence from me, and I'd been on a path of destruction ever since.

He snatched my purse off the dresser and rummaged through it before dumping its contents onto the floor.

"Yo, bruh, you trippin'. You need to take your crackhead ass out my room," I said, pushing him out the way and bending down to pick up my belongings before he gave me a backhanded smack.

I held my stinging cheek and started backing away from him. That shit had me spooked out.

"Where the money at? I need it!" he barked, looking under my pillow and discovering nothing. He turned toward me so I could see the desperation on his face. He suddenly pulled a knife out of his pocket.

"I don't have any money," I pleaded as I looked back and forth between him and the knife. I had to figure out how to at least get out of his way so I could call for help.

He walked up to me and stuffed his hand down my bra. Tears threatened to fall down my face as I felt his dirty, grimy hands circle around my nipple. He removed his hand but kept the knife pointed at me as he pulled down his dirty sweatpants.

"No," I sobbed.

"Yeah, pucker up, you little dirty bitch," he said while pointing his scrawny, scribbled up dick in my face. I started gagging from the awful-ass stench coming from his balls.

"Why are you doing this?" I asked to waste time. I was hoping somebody, anybody, would come in and save me.

"Dad, what you doing?" a deep voice asked.

Harry turned around with his dick still out. "Frederick, what you doing here, boy?" he asked, quickly pulling up his pants.

I'd missed seeing Rico's handsome-ass face, but I didn't focus on it. I got up and grabbed as much shit as I could. I planned on leaving, and I wasn't coming back.

"I came to see if you was good. I ain't heard from you in a minute. You look bad, mane," Rico stated, looking at his father in disgust.

Nobody knew that Rico was my step-brother, because Rico didn't claim Harry. Explaining that to people that didn't know us would have been a waste of time.

"I'm good, little nigga. I'm your daddy," Harry chuckled as he patted Rico on the shoulder. As he leaned in closer, I heard him whisper, "You got that for me?"

I snapped my head in Rico's direction as he patted his pockets down before digging in his jacket and pulling out a clear plastic bag with white rocks inside.

"Good looking out." Harry tried to grab the bag, but Rico snatched it away.

"And don't go asking around for me. According to these niggas, I don't got a father," he stated coldly before tossing Harry the bag.

Harry looked like a kid on Halloween. I was relieved when I saw him dash out my room. The front door slammed shut moments later. Next, I had to face the monster's son.

Chapter 20

Rico

"You good?" were the only words I could muster. I didn't expect to see my pops tryna molest Eboni. It felt like we were kids all over again.

He used to make us touch and fuck each other while he touched himself. After a while, I got too old, but Eboni actually liked me and felt I was her protector. That shit had my mental all the way fucked up. For a minute, I thought about blowing his brains out and helping Eb get far away from that fucked-up ass house.

"Yeah," she said, looking spaced out. I could tell she was grateful, but at the same time, I had to see where her head was at.

"E, I need a favor," I said as I plopped down on her bed, trying to erase the images of what happened moments prior. That shit was sick. He raised her since she was a little girl. For him to try some bogus shit like that, high or not, was foul.

"What is it?" She sniffled a little and wiped her face as she stuffed her bags.

I was quiet as I contemplated whether I could trust her to keep her fucking trap shut.

She turned to me with a raised brow.

"Come sit next to me, 'cause this is some serious shit I want you to do for me," I said, patting a seat next to me on her messy, twin-sized bed.

She hesitated a little before sitting next to me. I decided to put her up on my little master plan.

"What?" she sassed.

I knew she wanted to get outta there before everyone came and she would have to explain her reasons for leaving.

"I need you to help me set up Teyanna's new nigga," I said with a straight face.

A devilish grin appeared on her face. "What? Why?"

"Listen, Tey ain't gon' be happy with no nigga but me, and since she keep trying to floss that nigga in my face, I think it's time to bring out the big guns. She fucked over the wrong nigga, on dawgs." I left out the part where, after I murked Terror, I would console Tey, and she would have no choice but to give a nigga a second chance.

"Okay, cool," Eboni said.

She agreed so easily that my mind started to wander. Then again, her ass probably had been thinking about some shit she wanted to do.

"That's it?"

"Yeah, if that's what you need me to do," she said, standing up and grabbing her bags.

"Wait, where you going?"

Eboni had no real family and no money to make it on streets alone. That was one of her problems. She ain't think shit out before she did it.

"I don't know, Rico, but I know one thing: I can't stay here. Did you see your father? That nigga is a fucking animal!"

"Watch your fucking mouth, my nigga. That ain't my father." I cringed, hearing him being called that. Nobody knew that sherm head was my dad. Even as a kid, when he started tweaking, I made sure to stay away from him. Well, my mom did once I hit sixth grade.

"Whatever, I'm out," she said, chucking the deuces and walking out.

I heard the front door open and shut. I sat there and put my face into my palms as I thought about how I was gonna kill Terror and anybody who got in my way. After a couple more minutes, I looked around and noticed how nasty the room really was with roaches crawling up and down the walls and jumping off the ceiling. I scoffed and walked out the house undetected before anyone showed up.

As I walked out of the project building, I thought about my own home situation. I hadn't been back home since that night. I knew I would have to go back soon. I wasn't feeling sleeping on my cousin's couch. Shit was fucking up my neck and back.

I needed to relieve some stress. I pulled out my phone, dialed a number, and waited for someone to answer.

"Isis speaking," he answered after the second ring.

"Wassup, baby?" I asked, trying to sound sexy. I was in need of some ass right now, and since I knew Eboni wasn't in the mood to give it up and Teyanna was out of the question, I decided to hit up the next best thing.

"Oh, wassup, love? You miss me?" he said in a sweet feminine voice.

"Something like that," I chuckled. I just wanted to catch the neck again and maybe get my asshole slurped on a little bit. Other than that, I was good.

"So why don't you slide through and bless me with that dick, daddy."

"Alright, I'll be there in ten."

"Okay, I'll be ready," he said before hanging up.

I was ready to slide into something tight, wet, and warm.

.

Chapter 21

Omniscient

alking through the side entrance of the warehouse, Terror and Bishop checked their phones once again to make sure that they were powered off. They were all the way in New Jersey, but wanted to be extra cautious because the shit that was about to go down couldn't be linked back to them. On the inside, Terror was on edge; he even had a half-pint Hennessy bottle in his hand.

"Yo, T," a nigga by the name of K.G. called out, but Terror ignored him.

He was on a mission to kill.

Bishop slapped palms with a few niggas. Everyone had it right. Bishop was the loose cannon, but Terror was deadly. He had gotten the name Terror from torturing muthafuckas before he killed him. His silence was loud, and his all-black clothing only displayed how serious shit was about to get.

He stood in the front and waited for the thirty-plus men present, his most trusted soldiers, to shut the fuck up. He hadn't even wanted to come out in broad day, but since he had other shit to tend to, he was gonna torture Don until he got the answers he wanted and then kill him.

"Where Don at?" Terror asked, taking a swig of the bottle before screwing the top back on.

"Behind you," Bishop said, pointing to the plain wall.

Two of the younger soldiers pushed the hidden doors disguised as a wall. Terror waited patiently as he watched the doors open, revealing a badly-beaten and bloody Don hanging right-side up. He was barely conscious and was butt naked. Two of Don's workers were sitting naked in metal chairs but not as badly beaten.

Terror eyes lit up with excitement. He passed the bottle to Bishop and walked over to where the biker chains laid on the ground.

"No, T, man please. I'll get the money back. Don't do this," Don cried. He knew there would be no leaving there alive. He wondered why he let someone convince him that it would be easy to fuck Terror over.

Terror looked at the nigga he once called a friend. One thing he was not about to do was show mercy. One could hear the chains drag on the hard concrete as Terror circled the room until he faced Don's back. "Yo' ass really thought you could steal from me?"

Whap! Whap! Whap! Whap!

"Aarghhhhhhhhhhhhh!" Don screamed.

Niggas had to turn their heads as blood squirted and gashes opened on Don's back. Bishop looked on in amazement. He loved when his cousin got like that.

"All y'all muthafuckas need to look, 'cause this what's gon' happen to the next nigga that think shit is sweet enough to steal from us," Bishop said, walking over to where Terror stood. He untwisted the cap off the Hennessy bottle, took a swig, and threw some on the open wounds on Don's back and head.

Don's back was badly cut. They could see his white meat.

"Shut up and stop being a little bitch. You'll be a'ight," Terror said, his voice calm. He walked over to the two guys tied up in the metal chairs and pulled out his chrome revolver.

He shot the chunkier, shorter guy first. Terror didn't even flinch as the man's brains splattered against the ground and his body slumped. He shot the other guy once between the eyes. Some of the men looked like they wanted to shit themselves. They knew how Terror was. That was why they didn't think about crossing him.

Terror went back over to Don and slapped him with the butt of his gun.

"Who put you up to this? I promise I'll make your death quick and painless," he said with a laugh so sinister that it scared some of the toughest dudes there to the core.

Don spit out the blood in his mouth. He felt like his jaw was dislocated. "Suck my dick. I ain't telling you shit, you fraud-ass nigga." He hawked up as much spit as he could and spit in Terror's face.

Terror smiled and nodded as he wiped his face. "That's your word?" he asked, staying cool, calm, and collected.

Don didn't answer, but it didn't matter. Terror was gonna make sure he regretted it before he deaded him.

"Yo, Eli, he said suck his dick, bro," Terror said.

His young bull Eli emerged from the group of men, pulling out a hunting knife so large it made Don's eyes damn near pop out of his head. He started squirming around, trying to free himself, but it was pointless.

Eli walked up, grabbed Don's dick, and cut it off in one swift motion.

Don yelled out like a wounded animal. It didn't sound like any noise a human would make.

Eli shoved the penis in Don's mouth.

A few of the guys laughed as they watched the most savage shit occur. There were a couple of 'Damn sons' heard, but nobody felt bad. He'd done it to himself with his greed.

"Well, gentlemen, this concludes today's meeting," Terror said as he lit a match and tossed it on Don, who instantly caught on fire.

One guy threw up, making Terror laugh as he walked over to where Truth was and patted him on the shoulder.

"Have these niggas clean it up. I'll get up with you later," Terror said, leaving with Bishop not too far behind him.

"Alright, boss," Truth said, taking over the show. "Y'all niggas clean this shit up!"

A few men fell out of line to follower the order.

Once they were back inside the truck, Bishop spoke.

"Cuz, what the fuck was that? I thought you was done getting your hands dirty," he said, still excited about having seen his cousin murk somebody.

"Yeah, I know what I said, but niggas thought it was a game." Terror started the engine. "I'm hungry, though, and we ain't going to my mom's house for a couple hours." He pulled off and drove smoothly, careful not to draw attention to himself.

$\infty \ \infty \ \infty$

In NYC

The girls were at the Dominican salon getting their hair done.

"What did you want again, mami?" the heavyset stylist asked as she ran her hands through Teyanna's hair.

"I want a wash and set, but I also want my hair colored. Just the tips." Teyanna sat back and watched the lady through the mirror.

"What color?" the lady motioned for Tey to sit at the sink.

"Like an orangey-brown."

Taj was already under the dryer, and Lo was getting her extensions clipped in.

"So what y'all wearing tonight?" Tey asked.

"I don't know, but we can't go in there looking any ol' type of way or looking like some damn strippers, so I guess we should go shopping!" Lo spoke.

"Well, I ain't bring any clothes so shopping, it is! We need to get some food, too, 'cause I'm hungry as hell." Tey rubbed her growling stomach.

"Shit, me too," Taj agreed.

"Tey... Taj."

Out of nowhere, Lauren spoke up in soft, innocent voice, so the girls knew it was some bullshit. They gave her their attention, anyway, because they were curious as to what had her acting all timid and shy.

"I have to tell y'all something," Lo said, fidgeting with her nails.

"Oh, Lawd, what is it now?" Tey asked.

"Yes, girl, what?" Taj laughed, shaking her head. They had no idea what was gonna come out that crazy girl's mouth.

"Well, y'all know Nas and I been together for a long time, and we been having our issues," Lo said with her head down.

"Yes, we know. Now get to the point, bitch!" Taj said.

"Well, I stepped out and met someone new, and I'm really feeling this person. We been talking for a minute now, and I think it's time that we made it official."

"Why are you playing with us, Lo? I'm about to get out this chair and pop your ass! Get to the point! Who is this mystery man? Do we know him?" Tey asked.

Lauryn inhaled like she was smoking a fat-ass blunt before exhaling slowly. She looked at them both and finally spoke.

"Bishop," she said with a smirk.

Tey and Taj looked at each other and laughed.

"See told you!" Tey said, giving Taj an air high-five and leaving Lo confused.

"Wait. Huh?" Lo said.

"Now your ass owe me twenty dollars," Tey said, shrugging.

The stylist proceeded to add the hair dye to the ends of Tey's hair, making her clench up.

Lo looked at Taj, who continued laughing as the lady who was doing her hair took out the rollers.

"You know what? I'm not even gonna ask. Anyways, enough about me. How y'all two little boos doing?" Lo asked, trying to change subject and avoid the third degree.

"I don't know. Gina is too damn clingy. I mean, I love her, but she does the most. Not to mention, my dad is getting suspicious. I know I'm gonna eventually have to tell him," Taj said with a sad look.

Tey and Lo felt bad because that was their sister, yet there was nothing they could do to fix the situation.

"I say cut her off and get you some dick, girl," Lo spoke bluntly, making Tey's eyes buck as others listened to their conversation.

Taj was embarrassed. "I'm good, I like what I got," she said, waving Lo off, though a small part of her was starting to miss a man's touch.

"Hmm, that's not what it sounds like. But anyways let's talk about Teyanna hot ass," Lo said, turning to where Tey was sitting.

"Umm, let's not. Thank you," Tey said, rolling her eyes. She hated to broadcast her business, especially around people she didn't know. But Lauryn was a Gemini, meaning she didn't give a fuck about people's opinions; she was gon' do and say whatever she wanted.

"We know Terror putting that pipe down right. He got you looking thicker than a Snicker right now," Lo taunted as she and Taj snickered.

Taj was happy the attention wasn't on her relationship with Gina. She wasn't all the way open about her sexuality yet. At times, she still questioned it.

Unbeknown to them Brianna, Terrence's old flame, was soaking everything up like a sponge. Her blood boiled as she sat next to her cousin, Mercedez, who just shook her head. They both knew there was only one Terror they could have been referring to.

"But you gotta give Tey her props, though. You see we got one of his big boy toys today, driving around in style," Taj boasted as if she was the one who was Terror's.

Brianna had heard enough and was ready to get up and blackout on those dumb little girls. They were fucking up her day by talking about someone she considered her man and was deeply in love with. She wanted her man back, even if it meant beating up his new girl and possibly killing her.

Chapter 22

Brianna

I walked out the salon on ten. I tried my hardest to mask it; I couldn't let Mercedez see a bitch in her feelings. I had to keep my cool and act unbothered. I loved my cousin. She was cool, but she ran her mouth too much.

"Bitch! Was that your man they were talking about back there?" Cedez asked while trying to catch up with me as I walked to the nearest train station.

"Nah," I said, aggravated because there that trout mouth-ass hoe was, trying to instigate some shit.

"There's not that many niggas named Terror, and it looked like ol' girl was pushing his V."

I stopped walking and turned to face her. A bitch wanted to beat the living shit out of Cedez, but my beef wasn't with her.

"Listen, Cedez, and listen clearly: I don't wanna talk about that bullshit, so dead it." I began walking down the steps.

"Son, you ain't gotta be disrespectful," she huffed.

I rolled my eyes, not even entertaining her with a response.

To keep it a buck, I was ready to put a bullet in little shawty's skull and reclaim my man. Mark my words, nobody was coming between us, and whoever thought they would was gon' get sent straight to their maker.

We got down to the train stop, and I searched through the pockets on my Marmot coat for my pass so I could push through the turnstile.

"Bri, lemme get a swipe; I lost my card," Cedez begged.

I just rolled my eyes and passed the pass off to her as I went through. That bitch was broke and forever begging. I mean, I ain't have much of shit, just the few stacks

Terror used to give me every now and again. That shit was starting to dry up fast. I needed a hustle, but I had no idea what.

Two transfers later, we were back at my apartment in Red Hook. I stayed to myself, so I wasn't tryna be out there like that. Cedez ain't really have nowhere to go until I let her stay on my couch, and she turned to stripping. From what I saw, she brought in a decent amount of change every now and again. I just couldn't see myself doing it. Personally, I thought she was selling pussy on the side.

"You want me to pick up Dooda from downstairs," she asked, mentioning my five-year-old son, whom I adored.

His father, Semaj, was a lowlife, low-level weed dealer. I couldn't stand the ground he walked on. He fooled me. My naive ass thought I had a ballin'-ass nigga. At fifteen, I was very gullible. He told me he loved me, sold me a dollar and a dream, and basically gave me his ass to kiss when I told him I was pregnant. After that, my mother kicked me out.

I did it all alone. I was the one who had to fuck and suck to earn every dime. Welfare paid the bills, and that was about it. I still needed clothes and shoes for me and my baby. I still saw Semaj around the way. He had ten kids, last I heard, and took care of none of 'em.

"Yeah, you can, and I'ma just start dinner," I said, walking into the kitchen. I couldn't help but look around in disgust. Mercedez was the definition of a slob. She ain't know how to clean up behind herself. Shit, she barely even washed her ass. I remembered once I was up at the club, supporting her, and niggas said she smelt like fish and rotten ass. I was so embarrassed.

Apparently, she was too, 'cause she quit that night and began working at another club not too long afterwards.

I decided to give my hubby forever a call, making sure I called private.

Ring, ring, ring.

I lightly tapped my foot as I waited for him to answer. I couldn't help but wonder if he was with that bitch that was jacking him at the hair salon.

"Yo."

I could sense he was frustrated. I should've just hung up, but it was like the nigga had me hooked, and I took him anyway I could have him.

"I miss you," I cooed.

"Da fuck you want, Brianna? Now ain't the time," Terror said.

I could tell he was trying to keep his cool.

"You," I stated, not even giving one fuck about none of that attitude he had. I had the antidote for all that. I missed daddy, and I was sure he missed me.

"Check it, ma: I got a shorty. Stop checking for a nigga," he said coolly.

"Oh, you mean 'Tey,'" I said, chuckling a little. I knew that nigga had a million and one questions.

"How the fuck—"

"I saw that little bitch of yours with her ugly-ass friends. Don't worry. I was a good girl. I ain't tell her nothing."

"There ain't nothing to tell. Your ass delusional, B."

Right when he said, that Mercedez walked in holding a very tired Brandon's hand.

"Okay, Terror, baby. I love you, too. I'll call you later. Bye." I threw in Terror's name just because I knew Mercedez's nosey ass was listening, and then I ended the call.

Chapter 23

Terror

I sat in the basement that was decked out with a bar, a pole, a flat screen, and a black, leather La-Z-Boy. I was a little bent off the Henny, but not to the point that I ain't know that I stopped talking to the bitch over three months ago.

"Bruh, she still on your body?" Bishop questioned, laughing and holding his stomach.

"That shit ain't funny," I said, taking a few pulls too many on the L. I could tell that he was about to say something by the look he gave me. He had me damn near ready to laugh.

"Damn, nigga, you gonna hog the blunt all day or what? It's puff, puff, pass."

I sucked my teeth and passed him the blunt.

"I ain't stressed. That bitch need to move the fuck around."

My phone began to ring again. It was from an unsaved 718 number, so I assumed it was my soon to be ex-connect.

"Hello," I said.

"Terrence, mi boi. Long time, mi not hear." Glen's heavy Jamaican accent blared through the phone.

"What's good, G? You in the city?" I asked while looking over at Bishop, who had an unsure look on his face.

"Yessir, mi outside. Don't keep mi waiting too long," he said before ending the call.

My ass was nervous, pissed off, and confused as to why in the fuck he was there. Niggas knew not to pop up at my crib unannounced. I ain't give a fuck how powerful that goat-eating muthafucka was. Not a damn thing was stopping me from letting him know.

∞ ∞ ∞

"What's good, G?" I slid into the back of the Suburban. Bishop was strapped and guarding my side of the door. I had only met G a few times. I could count the meetings on my fingers. I nodded at his son, Sylvester, who was cooler than his punk-ass daddy.

"I heard through di grapevines you don't want to do business anymore," Glen said, getting straight to the point.

"Well, your grapevines is right, G. I found someone offering better product and better prices. Only a fool would turn that down."

"That's not a wise idea," he said, sitting back and speaking calmly.

"No disrespect, but that's my choice. You popping up at my crib ain't a wise idea, fam, and I don't appreciate it." At the end of the day, I was a grown-ass man, and he wasn't about to check me like some little ol' bitch. I was thirty-eight hot.

"Okay, I hear you. I take it you'll have mi money in seventy-two hours." He pulled out a cigar, examined it, and lit it before blowing smoke in my direction, which I thought was disrespectful and done intentionally.

"Yeah, set up the drop-off and I'll get you that." I knocked on the window, letting Bishop know to let me out.

"Tree days, no excuses, mi boy," he yelled before the door closed.

I jogged back across the street to my house, looking around to make sure there weren't any nosey-ass neighbors looking outside or nothing out of the ordinary.

"What was that shit about?" Bishop started firing off questions.

I wasn't even in the mood to drink or smoke anymore as we went to the kitchen. I grabbed a water bottle and took a sip.

"T, what that nigga say? Do I have to call a meeting?" Bishop asked. He seemed shook by my silence.

"Nah, we just gon' give Glen his bread back and make moves with that nigga, Chino," I spoke calmly, but I ain't really know if Glen was gon' try some snake shit. I would have to have a backup plan in case shit went left.

"His money? Did you forget that ol' boy stole a lot of that shit? Do you got bread to replace that?"

I twisted my lips to the side and gave Bishop the illest mug, like he had asked some despicable shit.

"My fault, B."

I took another sip of the water, trying to sober up as quickly as possible.

"He said we got three days," I announced, making Bishop's mouth drop. "Don't worry,. I got the guwop, but we gonna need some of our soldiers there when we do the exchange. I don't trust this nigga."

"A'ight, my nigga. What you wanna do in the meantime?" he asked, looking to me for some type of guidance.

Shit, I ain't know my damn self, but I wouldn't let him know that.

"We gon' play everything cool. We don't need the girls freaking out and shit. We going to my ma's house tonight. Keep on your A-game, though," I said, running my hands down my face just as the front door opened and shut.

Chapter 24

Tey

"Baby," I sang, entering the house, followed by the girls. We had stopped by the mall to pick up a few things. I had the new color in my hair with some candy curls and decided to buy me and bae a few matching outfits like the cute IG couples did.

"In the kitch—"

He stopped mid-sentence upon seeing me.

"Wow, look at you, sis." Bishop's mouth dropped, then his eyes widened at the sight of Lo's sexy ass. His eyes almost popped out of his head. Taj came in fucking clutch too.

I slowly took my time walking over to my man, who was hungrily eyeing me down.

"You like it?" I asked, breaking the silence as he continued to probe me with his eyes.

"I love it." He grabbed my hand and spun me around.

"You look good as fuck," he said, kissing my lips and grabbing my ass.

"Thank you." I tried to pull away, but he pulled me back in.

"Uh uh, where you going?" he growled in my ear with his deep, sexy, voice.

I started to feel moist, but I had to pull myself together. We couldn't go there. We had to be at his mom's house in an hour, and I wasn't trying to fuck up my new style and risk not going to meet the future in-laws.

"To finish getting ready, baby. Remember, we supposed to go have dinner at your mom's."

He paused for a second. I could feel him smiling and what he said next sent chills down my spine. "I mean, we can reschedule that." He kissed my neck and then my shoulder.

"I'm wit' you on that one, T," Bishop said as he looked Lo up and down as she posed for another selfie.

"Nooo, I wanna go," I whined, poking out my bottom lip.

"Alright," Terrence said, throwing his hands up in defeat. "Go get ready before I change my mind." He gave my ass one good smack.

"Owww, muthafucka, that hurt," I said, running into the foyer, taking the stairs two at a time. I was excited and nervous to meet the in-laws.

∞ ∞ ∞

"Are you ready?" Terrence asked, lightly shaking my thigh.

I turned, giving him a half smile and nodding my head. Taj, Bishop, and Lo rode in a different car, but they were there as well.

"Don't worry, baby, my family gon' fuck with you. I don't bring girls home," he said, smiling and causing me to smile.

I felt special.

He held my hand as we walked up the stairs to the castle-like house. Drawing in a deep breath, I watched as he knocked on door. A few moments later, a lady answered the door. I assumed she was his mother, Patricia.

She was gorgeous. She had a chocolate complexion that was smooth like she bathed in cocoa butter and melanin magic, and she had curly, jet-black hair just like Terrence.

"Oh, my Lawd, have mercy. My baby is here," she yelled, pulling Terrence into her embrace.

I couldn't help but admire their bond.

"I missed you, Mommy," Terrence said, towering over his mom as they rocked side to side while hugging.

"I missed you, too, boy," she said, grabbing his face and looking into his eyes. She let go of him and walked up to me with the biggest smile she could muster, which caused me to cheese so hard, I felt like my cheeks were going to fall off.

"You must be Teyanna," she said, pulling me into a tight, motherly embrace. "You look gorgeous, chile."

"Thank you, Ms. Pat," I said, hugging her back. Terrence told me that was what everyone called her.

"You can call me Mama Pat. After all, you are the only young lady Terrence has brought home to meet me." She gave him an approving smile before refocusing on me.

"I've heard so much about you, honey. Do you know how to cook?"

"Yes," I said shyly.

"Alright, come on. You can help me and Gia in the kitchen."

I removed my jacket, and Terrence took it as I went to the sink to wash my hands. He kissed my cheek.

"I'll be in the living room with the guys and the kids until the food is done."

I nodded before turning my undivided attention to his mama as we got busy in the kitchen.

While laughing and getting to know more about each other, I found out that babe was African American, Panamanian, and Puerto Rican. He had three siblings. Gia, who was the oldest and damn near fifteen years older than Terrence, who was the baby. After Gia came Derrick. He was thirty and had four beautiful kids with his wife, Crystal. Next was Jonathan, who was five years older than Terrence. He had just gotten his degree in engineering, had a good job working on cars, and even owned his own business.

Lo, Taj, and Bishop had finally joined us for dinner. It seemed like Jonathan couldn't keep his eyes off Taj, but she wasn't paying him any mind at all.

Babe's mom really had us throw down like we were having some type of feast. She had all the good Panamanian dishes, and none of 'em disappointed my taste buds at all. She made chicken tamales, *arroz con pollo*, which was chicken and rice, and pernil. It was all good, but that pernil was hitting the spot, so I decided to get more.

"Girl, you so tiny. Where all that damn food going?" Terrence's mom asked, causing everyone to laugh.

"My baby can eat," Terrence said.

I couldn't help but to giggle and shake my head. I had been feeling hungrier lately, and that food was just what I needed.

"I'm sorry, but it tastes so good. I can get used to this. I wiped the corners of my mouth and took a few sips of the juice Mama Pat had made. I was hype because I had her write up all the recipes and all the ingredients I would need so I could make the dishes at home.

Terrence and I had been dating for such little time, yet we'd found something in each other that had been missing.

"I can't believe my son has a girlfriend," his mom said, still in shock.

I mean, was he really a playboy? If so, I couldn't believe little ol' me from Boston made a Brooklyn nigga change his ways and settle down.

The rest of dinner went great. Gia, me, Taj, Lo, and Gia's friend Jackie hit it off and decided to hit the strip club up while the guys stayed home and played the game. We lied because we knew they weren't letting us out the door if they knew where we were going. We just said to the club, which wasn't technically a lie.

"So, sis, how come Crystal ain't come?" I asked.

Crystal seemed cool, but neither Ms. Pat nor Gia acknowledged her. She kept urging Derrick to go, but it seemed like he was enjoying himself too much.

Jackie sucked her teeth but seemed to be biting her tongue. She ain't say nothing as Gia began to break down how Crystal was a shiesty hoe and how she had to put her hands on her more than once for touching Derrick or fucking up his car.

"Oh my God," I said, cupping my mouth as Taj and Lo listened from the back seat. One saying, "Damn," and the other just laughing. I bet it was Lo's disrespectful ass.

"Yeah, girl, plus Jackie got my niece by him." She and Jackie shared a laugh.

I shook my head and giggled at how messy they were, but I still fucked with them.

Once we pulled up, I was scared they wasn't gon' let us in 'cause me, Lo, and Taj were nowhere near twenty-one years old yet. Shit, we were barely eighteen. I guess Gia and Jackie were regulars, because we cut the line and got our hands stamped without them carding us.

When I tell you the strippers were fine as fuck, I mean it. Not to mention that they were fucking packing, but I knew the rule: look but don't touch.

I needed a drink; a good one. I planned on getting bent.

"Can I have an apple daiquiri, please?" I requested, sitting at the bar. My makeup had me looking older than I actually was, so it worked in my favor.

I paid for my drink and took a sip. I could feel somebody's eyes on me, and I turned to see a fine-ass dark-skinned dude with some neat-ass dreads gliding his way over to me. He sat at the empty barstool next to me, licking his lips and glaring at my body. I reminded myself I was happy and couldn't entertain the handsome stranger invading my space.

"Hey, gorgeous," he said, showing off his perfect pearly whites.

Oh, gawd.

I took another sip of my drink. The shit wasn't strong enough, though. Maybe I should've ordered some Henny straight.

"Oh, you don't speak?" the sexy, mysterious man asked, chuckling.

"No, I don't talk to strangers." I stood up.

He grabbed my hand, causing me to snatch away and frown.

He put his hands up in defense. "I'm sorry, little mama. I ain't mean no disrespect." He stuck his hand out for me to shake. "I'm Quincy." Even in a dark club, I could tell his chocolate ass had it going on. It was kinda suspect how his ass was walking around a male strip club, though, but I was taken, so I wasn't about to question a damn thing.

My drink in my left hand, I stuffed my clutch under my arm and put out my right hand for him to shake. He held it too long, which caused me to pull away.

"Teyanna," I mumbled.

Wait, why in the fuck did I tell this nigga my real name?

Nigga could've been a stalker or something.

"Well, tell me something, Ms. Teyanna. What's a baddie like you doing at the strip club alone?"

I laughed at his corniness. "I'm not. I'm here with my girls, but you stepped in my way."

"I'm sorry, hun. I was just tempted to come over here and talk to you." He winked, and we both chuckled.

"Thanks, but no thanks, Quincy. I have a man. I'll see you around."

Once I made it over to the VIP section where the girls were seated, I saw that they were all enjoying the two strippers that were dancing. Boy, did they look tasty. Not as tasty as Mr. Quincy, but they would have to do.

"Bitch, where was you at?" Taj yelled over the loud music while sliding a bunch of ones in the Spanish stripper's Jock strap. She seemed to be enjoying the guys' dancing way too much.

I really thought that bitch had been delivert. She barely talked about Regina's ass the whole weekend. I was gon' see what was up with that. Who knew? She would probably find herself a nigga and stop doing all that gay shit.

"I went to get a drink from the bar," I said, lifting up my glass so she could see my drink before I threw the whole thing back. It went down smooth, but I was ready to drink some liquor. Just in the nick of time, the bartenders delivered a bottle of Ace of Spade.

Chapter 25

Lo

"And the moment all you ladies been waiting for... are y'all ready to get punished?!" The DJ announced as a whole bunch of horny ladies pushed each other around.

The dancer Punisher came to the stage in his Egyptian king getup or whatever. He did look scrumptious, though.

"That's Quincy," Tey slurred, pointing at the guy on stage. Tey ain't even drink like that, but she managed to drink two sour apple Daiquiris, Henny, Alizé, and a couple shots of Ace of Spade. All the girls were done. I was pretty sure Terror's sister wasn't driving. She said something about calling her fiancé to come and get us. Jackie was already laid up on the sofa knocked out, and Taj was Snapchatting everything. It was too lit, though. I was enjoying myself.

"Girl, who?" Gia questioned, giggling. She'd responded like two minutes too late.

"Shhhh," Taj said as she recorded the guy on stage. "Songs on 12 Play" by Chris Brown and Trey Songz was playing as the stripper got off the stage and made his way over to our section. The spotlight followed him.

He had every female's attention, including mine, but his eyes stayed focused on my girl Tey. She tried avoiding contact, but he lifted her out of her seat.

"No, no, no," Tey protested.

Her pleas were ignored as she became the center of attention. He seemed to be dead set on getting her. The crowd of horny drunk women roared in excitement.

"You better get it, bitch," Gia chanted as Punisher picked Tey all the way up and carried her to the stage.

I watched in anticipation for his next move as she stood on stage nervously.

"Look, my mans, P, got little mama shook," the DJ said over the microphone.

Punisher told Tey to lay down on the longue chair, and she obeyed. Everyone watched him crawl between her legs. He slithered his tongue like a snake at the crowd, making the ladies go wild. Then, he buried his face between her legs and slid his way up her body 'til they were pelvis to pelvis. He started grinding to the beat.

You would think they were fucking, the way Punisher's body was moving against hers, as he began to lift her leg, still grinding to the beat. He leaned down, licked her ear, and whispered into it.

With her leg in the air, he maneuvered her little body around on the chair until she was face down, ass up. He began to lightly pull on her hair as the crowd roared, throwing wads of money on the stage. Even Gia and Taj went up front and center and threw some bills.

"Goddamn," I spoke as I watched in admiration. That chocolate god knew how to work his hips. Jackie's ass even began to wake up, and when she did, her eyes damn near bugged out her head.

"Bitchhhh," she shrieked as she dug around in her purse before the song could come to an end. She stumbled her drunk ass over to the stage area and threw some ones as Punisher lifted Teyanna up in the air and slammed her against his pelvis. I saw Tey letting loose and letting him have his way.

Once the song was over, he went backstage and took Teyanna with him. She arrived at the table less than ten minutes later with a nervous grin on her face.

"Bitch, you did that!" Gia said, slapping fives. "You lucky my brother ain't here. That woulda made his yellow ass bug the fuck out," she joked, slapping fives with all of us as we joined her and began hyping up Teyanna, whose hair was sweaty and tied up in a ponytail.

"Oh my God, speak of the fucking devil," Jackie said, looking off.

We all looked at an angry Terror storming our way with Bishop and Jonathan not too far behind him. I knew there was about to be some shit. I looked at Tey, who looked like she was shitting bricks.

Chapter 26

Terror

I got a little scared after nobody answered my phone calls, but Brianna's sneaky ass managed to send me a video message from her new number of my girl basically dry fucking a nigga on stage. My blood was boiling. I ain't even think twice as I grabbed my keys and called Brianna so she could give me the exact address.

"A fucking strip club!" I barked on the phone to Bishop as I sped on the freeway, doing ninety and switching lanes. I ain't give a flying fuck about the cops. I wanted to fuck Teyanna's little ass up for doing dumb shit as soon as I let her out my sight.

I mean, yeah, a nigga still went to the strip clubs every once in a while and turned up with the bros, but she was my lady, and she was wildin' out if she thought she was gon' disrespect me.

I double parked in front of the club and hopped out. Bishop parked his V and got out. He had my sister's fiancé in the car, but he ain't come out. He was probably tryna calm himself down before he put his foot in her ass.

"Wassup, T?" the big bald security guard asked as I dapped him up, slapping a few Benjis in his palm, and made my way inside. The son of a bitch was packed.

"Hey, daddy," a few ladies said, pulling on my clothes as I walked past them, having to mush one of the thirst buckets that was tugging at my belt buckle. I spotted Teyanna and the girls sitting off in the VIP section without a care in the world.

Jackie spotted me first. She must've warned the rest of them, 'cause they all whipped their heads in my direction.

"Uh oh, I'm in trouble," Tey slurred as she began to giggle.

The other girls looked scared shitless. Gia's scary ass sunk lower into her seat. I was gonna get in her ass later 'cause this had her name written all over it. At that moment, I was gon' worry about getting my baby home.

"You bugging the fuck out, B," I snatched Teyanna up roughly by her arm.

"Stop, babe, you're hurting me," she whined.

Lo stood up to protest, but I wasn't in the mood to hear shit. "T, let her go. We were just having fun."

"Shut the fuck up and mind your business, my nigga. Let my mans handle that," Bishop said, blacking on Lo.

My eyes never left Tey. I was ready to beat the shit out of her, word to my muva.

"Let's go before I break my foot off in your ass," I threatened, gripping her arm a little tighter. I made sure not to apply too much pressure.

"No!" she slurred, snatching away. She continued as she began to cry, "You're being mean to me." She pouted as she sat back down, ignoring me and drinking that weak-ass Ace of Spade.

I got fed up with her antics, so I grabbed the bottle and tossed it with so much force it shattered on the ground. She wanted to cause a scene, so I was gonna give her one. I picked up Teyanna, slinging her small frame over my shoulder while she began to throw a tantrum like a big-ass child. I watched as Jonathan walked over to Taj's drunk ass as she struggled to stand up.

"Come on, ma. You falling over and shit. Lemme help," he said, catching her before she fell.

"I like pussy, Jonathan, okay?!" she slurred as he shook his head, picked her up bridal style, and carried her out. Gia and Jackie held each other up as they walked out.

Once we got to the truck, I opened the door, slid Tey into the passenger's seat, and walked around to get into the car.

"You bugging out, my nigga, dead-ass," I huffed as I peeled into traffic. I needed to spark a fat-ass blunt and clear my head before I went to jail behind Tey's ass.

"How? I was just going out to have fun. I don't say nothing when you and Bishop go out," she retorted.

I knew her little ass wanted to justify what she did, but there was no way around it.

"You also don't see me dry-fucking bitches in strip clubs, now do you?"

She shut her ass right up.

"Oh, that's what the fuck I thought. That little bullshit you pulled at the club tonight, son..." I spoke with my Brooklyn accent coming out a little too thick. I wasn't even able to finish what the fuck I had to say.

"Whatever. I don't even wanna talk about it," she slurred. "Just take me home."

We pulled into the driveway at the house. I ain't say another word to her on the ride back. Her ass was as drunk as a skunk, and I ain't have nothing else to say. I was big mad.

She got out the car, slamming the car door and almost breaking it.

"Ma, I'm not in the mood for your attitude and shit, so be careful when close my door," I warned.

"Nigga, fuck you and your door!" she stated before using her key and staggering into the house.

"Fuck is wrong with you, my nigga?" I said, grabbing her by her shoulder and spinning her around to face me.

"Fuck you, Terrence. Don't talk to me." She continued talking her shit but could barely walk, so I carried her up three flights of stairs, only for her to start again.

"Your ass probably cheating on me, anyways! You don't love me! You don't mean it!" she continued as she worked herself up.

I wasn't about to go there with her.

"Whatever, bruh, just stop talking to me with your drunk ass and go to bed!" I said, taking off my street clothes. I was ready to knock.

"I don't have to do a muthafucking thing," she walked up on me, pointing her fingers in my face.

"Alright, whatever. Do you." I laughed it off dismissively.

Less than five minutes later, Teyanna's face was in the toilet bowl. She had been throwing up and sobbing for a minute.

"Babe, help me; I'm dying," she cried out before throwing up again.

A nigga was pissed but still laughing my ass off. I held her hair and rubbed her back.

"Babeeeeeee." She wasn't throwing up but was still hanging on the bowl. "It's not funny. Something is wrong," she explained, crying.

"Yeah, you don't know your limits, T," I told her as she wiped her mouth with the back of her hand and used what little energy she had left to lift herself off the floor with my assistance.

She didn't say nothing else as she grabbed her toothbrush, toothpaste, and mouthwash. I grabbed a face rag and handed it to her. I watched her brush her teeth and gargle twice. She also made sure to wash the makeup and throw up off her face.

I had to help her bathe in the shower. After drying her off, I lathered her body up with lotion and put one of my shirts on her.

"Baby, I'm hungry," she whined, looking at me with pleading eyes.

"A'ight, I got you. Lay down." I made sure she was safely tucked in before I went downstairs and warmed up some food that I got from Mom's house.

I came back upstairs, and all hell broke loose when I found Teyanna in the bathroom with a mug so vicious, I was sure there was about to be some shit.

"Brianna? Who the fuck is Brianna, Terrence?" she barked with my phone in her hand.

"Fuck you doing with my phone, bruh?" I retorted, ignoring her question and reaching out for my phone, but I was too slow.

"Oh, so that's how we gon' play it?" she asked, throwing my phone into the toilet.

My first thought was to beat her ass, but I wasn't a nigga who hit females. I pinched the bridge of my nose, trying to count, but that shit wasn't working.

"Son! What the fuck?! You dead-ass?!" I snapped, grabbing Tey by her neck and slamming her against the wall. I balled up my first, but instead of punching her, I punched the wall, creating a big hole.

She looked frightened, and I realized I fucked up when she started shaking and sobbing like a big baby once I released her from my grip.

"Come on, ma, I'm sorry. I ain't mean that," I said, attempting to caress the side of her face as she moved away, still scared. I looked at her with pleading eyes. I ain't want my baby to ever think I would hurt her, especially not after all that she endured at the hands of her pussy-ass ex. I wanted to body that nigga from the moment she told me what happened on our first date.

"I'm not gon' hurt you, babe. I just let my anger get the best of me. I looked at my bruised knuckles, which were a little swollen. I felt like shit and feared I might've messed up what we had.

I slowly approached her, taking her into my arms and holding her as she cried. It broke a nigga's heart 'cause I promised I would never make her cry. I'd fucked up, and at that very moment, I was willing to do anything to make it right.

I leaned down and pecked her lips twice. "My fault, ma. You ain't gotta worry about no other female. I ain't checking for nobody but you," I said. "All that other shit is behind me, ma. I put that on everything." I sat her on the sink and looked deep into her eyes.

I could tell she was searching my eyes for a lie. Once she saw that there wasn't any, she wrapped her arms around my neck.

"I love you," she proclaimed before kissing me deeply.

"I love you too."

That shit was true, though. In the little time we'd been dealing with each other, I had already decided that I wanted her and only her.

I picked her up by her thighs and placed her on my shoulders. I was now eye-level with her pussy. I could smell the sweet scent it gave off. She grabbed my head for support as I placed her against a nearby wall and buried my face deep into her center.

"I'm sorry, Terrence. Baby," she cooed, running her fingers through my hair, massaging my scalp.

I began to French kiss her pussy and spell my name on her clit. I was sucking on that muthafucka for dear life too.

"Damn, ma, you taste good. You gon' cum in daddy's mouth, right?" My dick hardened as I feasted on her juicy fruit.

"Yessssss," she cried.

I could tell her ass was crying for real, too. Not to be cocky, but my head game had her damn near climbing walls.

"Cum, ma. Don't be scared," I said between licking and slurping on her hidden treasure like the shit was going out of style. Within minutes, I felt her body shake violently as I gripped her thighs tighter and continued sucking on her clit.

She was pouring her tasty juices into my mouth, and I drank up every bit.

I slowly let her down and carried her in my arms. I knew her legs weren't of any use just yet, and she looked damn near exhausted. God knew I loved the fuck out that girl. I made sure to prove that to her daily. She was the only female who could keep me happy. She wasn't after my pockets. Even though little momma could fuck up some commas, her love for a nigga was genuine. We were Terrence and Teyanna (TNT), and together, we blew shit up. I pulled her close, kissing her temple as her head rested on my chest, and she listened to my heartbeat as I ran my hands through her hair. I drifted off into a deep somber, reminding myself that I'd have to get a new phone the next day.

Chapter 27

Rico

"So, Frederick, have you been taking your medications? I believe it is"— my psychiatrist said, looking down at some papers before speaking again— "fifteen milligrams of Abilify in the morning, ten milligrams of Zyprexa twice a day, and two hundred fifty milligrams of Seroquel at night."

"Nah, I don't need it," I responded dryly. I ain't even know how those muthafuckas diagnosed me with level II bipolar disorder. I guessed my bullshit-ass momma did that. I'd had the diagnosis for years, though, since I was a little nigga. Nobody knew other than those that needed to know: my mom, my doctors, and my little bitch-ass brother.

I'd been home for a few days. After fucking Isis' faggot ass, a nigga went home. They had put out an active crisis alert on my ass and sent me right to the hospital, saying I was 'manic'. Ain't that 'bout a bitch? They could only hold me for seventy-two hours, but I had to talk to my psychiatrist, Dr. Sharon Garner.

"You know, Frederick, as part of your agreement to be released from Norfolk, you are supposed to take your medications as directed. If you do not comply with the stipulations, I'll have no choice but to contact the prosecutor," she said, writing something down on the notepad.

I couldn't do nothing but flex my jaw a little tighter and pray to God I ain't knock earth, wind, and fire out that bitch.

"That won't be necessary, Dr. Garner." My mom defended me against that ugly bitch all the time.

I, on the other hand, ain't give two fucks. I would disappear before she would be able to catch me.

"Listen, Mom, you don't need to beg her. If you want me to take 'em, I guess I can take 'em," I lied. That pug dog-looking bitch had me fucked up if she thought she was gonna use the police as a tactic to get me to bitch up, but I was gon' tell her what she wanted to hear.

"Good. I'll sign you off, and you can leave. I'll check up with you in three weeks. Please don't make me regret this," she said.

"Don't worry. You won't," I said, taking the papers and walking out the room. Ain't no-fucking-body telling me when and how to live my life. I was on a mission to kill Terror and get my baby back. Nobody was getting in the way of that. Not the law, not Eboni, and not Teyanna's bitch-ass friends.

And whoever tried would catch some hot ones.

Riding around looking for Tey was no easy task. She hadn't cut that whack-ass nigga, Terror, off yet. Just the thought of her being hardheaded had a nigga's blood boiling. I knew she had to be giving my pussy up to that sucker-ass nigga, which caused me to start beating the steering wheel while I sat at the stop light. I knew pedestrians and other drivers were looking at me like I was crazy, but I ain't give a fuck. As I wiped away the two tears that came down my face, I thought about how much I loved Tey. She was my sun, moon, and stars. I couldn't live life without her.

I dialed up a number and waited impatiently for an answer.

"Yes, Rico?" an annoyed Eboni said.

"Yeah, wassup with the drop on this dude?"

"Nobody knows, my nigga. It's like he's some type of fucking ghost!"

When I first told her I was gon' kill that nigga, Terrence, she warned me that I sounded dumb as fuck and said that nigga had enough money to have me killed and dispose of my body without a trace. I was heated as fuck. She was tryna play me like I was pussy.

"That nigga ain't no superhero or no shit like that; he can be touched." I spoke with confidence.

I was driving down a side street in Roxbury when two black SUVs cornered my car.

"Ughhhh, what the fuck?!" I yelled out of frustration. At the same time, I was shitting bricks. I wasn't packing my tooley, either.

Lo and behold, Terror hopped out the car, grinning from ear to ear.

"What? What's wrong?" a frantic Eboni screamed through the phone after hearing the commotion.

"I'll call you back." I hung up before she started giving me the third degree and watched as he walked up to my car.

I rolled down the window enough for us to see eye to eye but not enough for him to snatch me up or swing.

"I heard you were looking for me," he chuckled, strolling directly to the driver's side window.

"And if I was?" I said, matching his cocky-ass persona. In my eyes, that nigga ain't really have shit on me. Maybe Teyanna's gold digger ass was with him 'cause his pockets were longer than the underground railroad.

"This little nigga got heart," he said, laughing while turning toward his goons and then back to me.

"Listen here, son: stay away from my shorty. This is my first and final warning. I know where you and your whole family rest their heads, and I do mean your *whole* family," he warned with a serious look that gave me chills.

I knew that pretty muthafucka didn't play. Even though he had me shook, I reminded myself that Teyanna was mine, and I would lay down my whole life trying to get her back.

"I hear you," I responded.

He must've sensed I would still be chasing Tey.

"Don't just hear me. Understand me, because next time, shit ain't gon' be so sweet," he said before walking back to the truck, hopping inside, and closing the door. I waited until both SUVs drove off before pulling back onto the road. I needed that nigga gone like yesterday, and time was ticking, especially since he'd just threatened me.

Chapter 28

Teyanna

Two weeks later

I had been nauseous and sick to my stomach ever since we got back from New York. At first, I thought it was just a hangover. But after a day turned into days and days turned into weeks, I knew something was up. I thought I had some sort of food poisoning or stomach bug. Shit had gotten so bad that I finally decided after missing two days of classes that I was going to the doctor. I could only send in my reports via email for so long before they withdrew me from classes for absences.

I didn't want to go with anybody, but Lauryn's ass insisted she had to be there. Lord only knew what I would do without her and Taj; those bitches were my backbone. Terror wasn't that mad about the whole strip club situation anymore after he damn near tried to knock a bitch's head off. I'd never seen him that mad before, especially at me. I had to be careful, but that bitch's name— Brianna, I think it was— kept popping up.

"Teyanna Hunt," the heavyset Spanish nurse called.

Me and Lo stood up. Grabbing my purse, I inhaled . As I looked at Lo for reassurance, she gave me a warm smile and a small rub on my back.

"So, Ms. Hunt, I see that you've been having some abdominal pain and nausea. Have you been throwing up?" the nurse asked after introducing herself and putting on gloves.

"No," I said, sitting on the bed as she took my vitals.

"Everything seems to look good so far." She took the blood pressure cuff off my arm.

"Next, I'm gonna get your temperature and weight. Then, we can do some tests," she said, taking off her gloves and washing her hands.

My temperature was normal, but I had gained ten pounds. I mean, I ate, but I didn't think it was a lot. "When was your last menstrual cycle?"

I cringed at the question. I couldn't remember. The panic set in when I thought back to a couple weeks before, when my shit hadn't come. I looked at Lo, and she looked at me with a goofy-ass smirk spread wide across her face.

"I can't remember," I said, putting my head down.

"Don't worry, honey. We can do a pregnancy test. When was the last time you had intercourse?"

"Shitttt, she got some dick last night," Lo's ratchet ass blurted out.

I snapped my head in her direction so fast as she started laughing. She seemed amused by the thought of me being pregnant. The nurse laughed at Lo, but I ain't see a damn thing funny.

"Yesterday," I said shyly. I wasn't the type of female to brag about sex or even be open about having sex. I mean, I wasn't a saint, but I didn't feel comfortable sharing my sexual encounters, especially the ones with my baby. They were sacred. His dick game had me speaking in tongues and ready to commit a crime. I damn sure wasn't about to brag. You never know, a hoe may have tried to get at him, and I wasn't in no type of mood to be dragging bitches.

"See, that shit like crack to you. You can't get enough," Lo joked again.

That time, I gave her a death glare, letting her know to shut the fuck up.

"Well, Ms. Lady, let's take a test and see what's going on." The nurse gave me a clear container with an orange lid.

I pouted as I got up and dragged myself behind the lady, whose name, I learned, was Sandra.

I swear it took forever for me to pee. My ass was nervous, and then I began to ask myself questions.

What if I was pregnant? Would I finish school? Me and Terrence hadn't been talking that long. What would everyone think? Would Terrence still be around, and if not, would I be prepared to take care of my child alone? What would my parents think? I mean, my parents loved them some Terrence but a baby? I was only eighteen!

I finished peeing, wiped myself, and washed my hands before going back inside the room with Lo. She spoke, but I was too overwhelmed to talk.

The minutes seemed like hours. The results could potentially change not only my life but Terror's too.

There was a light knock at the door. In walked Sandra, wearing a nervous smile.

"So?" I spoke nervously.

"Well, missy, you're gonna be a mommy. Congratulations."

As soon as those words left her mouth, I felt like the wind had been kicked out of me. Lauryn was doing a happy dance in the corner, punching the air.

"I knew it! I knew it," she yelled.

The next half-hour of the appointment, we spent checking to see how far along I was. Sandra said six weeks and a day. She also informed me of the importance of eating and the dangers of smoking and drinking while pregnant. She gave me some pamphlets to look over as well as a prescription for prenatal vitamins and offered to answer any questions I had, but I didn't have any.

I was still in disbelief.

"Okay, Ms. Hunt, I will send over a referral to the OB-GYN for your first appointment. In the meantime, eat and get lots of rest. Congrats again, Teyanna. Don't be afraid to call if you have any questions," Sandra said, rubbing my shoulder.

I gave her a weak, one-sided smile, but I really just wanted to cry. I was basically a damn baby myself, and I was being told I was having one. I was scared shitless.

I was staying at Terrence's condo that night. I didn't know how I was gonna break the news to him. I didn't know if he would get angry or be happy, but it was time for me to put on my big girl panties, tell him what was up, and hope for the best.

Chapter 29

Terror

"Hey, sexy," I said, greeting my woman with a kiss as she entered the crib. I decided to treat Teyanna to a home-cooked meal. We had been going to restaurants a lot, and she had ended up getting sick as a result.

"Hi, baby."

I loved her sweet, little voice. Shit made a nigga's heart skip a beat. I could tell something was fucking with her, though.

"You good, ma?" I began fixing our plates. I made her some stew chicken with white rice and a side of beans, Panamanian style, of course.

"Yeah," she lied, giving me a big smile, but I could see straight through that fake shit.

I wasn't going to pressure her, though. I'd get to the bottom of it.

"I'm just asking. So how was your day, ma?"

"Nothing really. Me and Lo spent the day together." She turned her back to me and began washing her hands. I took this time to admire her round ass.

That shit had been getting fatter, thanks to me.

"Mhmm, you had fun?" I interrogated, walking up behind her, kissing on her neck, and turning her to face me.

"I guess. No, boy, get off me. I'm hungry," she said, nudging me, pushing past me, and sitting at the island.

"Well, let's hurry up and bust this shit down. I'm hungry too." I winked at her as she playfully rolled her eyes and started giggling.

"You nasty." She a big bite of food, closing her eyes to savor the taste.

"It's that good, huh?"

"Mmmm," she moaned, licking her lips and going in on the plate. She wasn't piggish with it, though. She could eat.

"Is it better than my mom's?"

"Boy, bye."

Tey loved her some of my mom, and my mom loved some Tey. They were always on the phone talking about going out to some damn nail salon or doing other girly shit that I ain't give a shit about. But I was happy that my two favorite ladies were getting along. Teyanna even texted and called Gia's ass occasionally, but Gia was either busy working or taking care of my grown-ass niece and nephew.

∞ ∞ ∞

"Ma, why you sitting all the way over there? Come here," I beckoned. Wifey asked to watch a movie but sat all the way on the opposite end of the couch, which was strange 'cause she usually wanted to lay up under a nigga and cuddle.

She slowly got up and sat next to me.

I picked *The Avengers,* and even though she ain't really care to see the movie, she sat there and watched it for a good hour until I decided to pause it and see what was up with her.

Sitting her on my lap, I just looked at her for a minute. "What's good, ma? You barely talked the whole night."

"Terrence, we have to talk," she stated, looking at the paused flat screen and avoiding eye contact.

"What's wrong?" I cupped her chin and turned her head to face mine. I could see that she wanted to cry. Something was really bothering my lady, and it was starting to bother me.

"I don't want you to be mad," she spoke as a couple tears slid down her face.

"I won't," I said, really unsure about if I would get tight or if it was some simple shit that babe was overexaggerating about. She took a deep breath and shifted her weight on my lap before she started.

"Well, I went to the doctor's today, and I found out I'm pregnant," she finished as more tears slid down her face. She lowered her head.

I lifted her face with my hands and kissed each eyelid before placing a passionate kiss on her lips. "I hope you ain't think a nigga would be mad at that," I said, wiping the rest of her tears.

"So you're not mad?" she said, looking up at me, confused, with puffy, red eyes.

"Why would I be?" I retorted, kind of pissed off she thought I'd be some slime-ass nigga.

"Because I don't want you to think I did this on purpose. I don't wanna trap you."

"Awww, girl, cut it out." I was gonna laugh, but her emotional ass would have probably cried more.

"I'm serious."

"Look at me, babe. You ain't gotta worry 'bout me thinking that. I got you and my seed. I'm a little excited you carrying a little me," I admitted, rubbing her flat stomach.

"Really?" she said, full of smiles.

"Hell yeah. Babe, we TNT."

"Aww, I love you," she said, leaning in, kissing me, and running her fingers through my hair.

"How much?" I lifted her by her ass cheeks and laid her on the sofa. I slid my shirt off as she looked at my chest then my eyes with nothing but lust in hers. I leaned down and kissed her before sliding her pants off and throwing them to the ground.

Chapter 30

Taj

"Taj... Taj! Do you hear me talking to you?" Gina yelled as we chilled in her room.

I was too distracted with texting. My hand had been glued to my phone since I got there the previous night. I didn't expect my friendship with Jonathan to blossom, but the longer I tried to hold it in, the more my attraction to him grew. There was only one problem: Gina

"I heard you," I said, rolling my eyes. It seemed like she wanted to forever be under me since I'd gotten back from New York. Or maybe I had just started to notice. I was ready to give her ass the boot. I ain't know how, though. Gina was a fighter and a damn good one. I would have to choose my words cautiously.

"So what I say, then?" she asked with her arms folded.

"Ummm—"

"Exactly, Natajah, you're full of shit. I swear to God, yo!"

We hadn't even had a good fuck session because, truth be told, I wasn't all the way there, and I believed she could tell.

"What you mean?" I asked, playing dumb as I tried to act mad and hop out the bed. I was gon' end the shit before I dragged her heart further through the dirt then I already had. I knew she ain't deserve that.

"You know exactly what the fuck I mean. You came here last night so we could spend more time together and get back to us, but here you are, smiling at texts and shit in my fucking face! How the fuck am I supposed to feel Taj? Huh?!" She began crying, but it wasn't a sad cry. It was more of an angry one, which started to scare me.

"Babe, listen, I—"

"Don't 'baby' me! You don't love me like I love you! I can tell with me is not where you wanna be, and as much as I hate this decision, I feel like it's my only one." She sniffled, wiping her snotty nose with the back of her hand. "I have to let you go so you can be happy with whoever you want, Taj."

I wanted to jump for joy, but I decided to play it cool and just look at her with a fake, pain-filled expression.

She walked closer to me. I flinched a little until she kissed my lips. That was her farewell to me.

She seemed too calm, and it felt awkward as fuck.

"I don't understand wh—"

"Just go. Taj."

I gave her one last saddened look and made my way out the door and down the steps on my way to my house. I honestly felt torn up about the whole situation, even though it went smoother than I thought it would. I had to call somebody and talk to them without feeling judged, so I called Johnathan.

"Hello, sweetheart." His smooth voice sounded caused my skin to redden. He made me feel something that I couldn't possibly describe.

"Hi, you." I lightened up a little.

"What's going on?"

I didn't know how he could sense something was bothering me. Maybe he should've went to school for psychology instead of engineering.

"Gina and I broke up," I said nervously. I was still in shock. I waited for a response, and what he said next kind of shocked me.

"How do you feel, love?"

"I honestly don't know how to feel," I answered. On one hand, I felt like crying, and on the other, I felt like a weight had been lifted off my shoulders.

"Well, just know I'm here for you. Whatever you wanna talk about, I'm all ears."

"I think I'm gonna be okay, but thank you so much," I said as I walked to my front steps.

"No problem, honey. But, aye, your girls are coming down today. Is there a possibility I'ma see you?"

I could hear the excitement in his voice.

"Maybe," I said playfully, opening the door. I saw my parents standing in the living room with sad looks on their faces. I held one finger up and finished up the call.

"Maybe? You playing games. I know your gorgeous self is coming, so be prepared to go on that date you owe me."

"Owe you? How you figure?"

"As I recall, I was the dude that brought your drunk ass home from a strip club."

He and I shared a laugh. He brought that up all that time.

"Alright, I got you, but you can't use that excuse all the time."

"I won't have to. I promise, after we go out, you'll want to see more of me."

"Okay, Mister Jonathan, whatever you say. But listen, I have to go and talk to my parents. I'll text you," I said. I hated having to end the call, but I knew I had to listen to what my parents had to say.

"Alright, beautiful. See you later," he said before hanging up.

"Hey, Mom. Hey, Dad. Wassup?" I took a seat on the couch.

"Hey, honey. We need to talk." My mom spoke in a tone that made me feel like something was wrong. I moved and sat at the table, where they were seated.

"What's wrong? What's going on?" I questioned, looking between both of them for answers.

They both grabbed one of my hands. My father looked up at me with pain in his eyes. I knew whatever was bothering him was hard for him to get off his chest. They were starting to scare me.

"It's Colleen," my father finally spoke.

Colleen was my birth mother. At that moment, I didn't know how to feel. I knew the worst had happened to her.

"She has stage four breast cancer, Taj, and she doesn't have much time left to live. She wants to see you," my stepmom said, searching my face for something.

I sure hoped it wasn't sympathy.

"Sorry, but I don't think that's a good idea," I said nonchalantly, pulling my hands away from both of them. I didn't want to see my birth mother. She had basically missed my whole life, and the memories that I had with her weren't all bad, but the bad was enough to outweigh the good.

"Please, Taj, just talk to her. Pray and find it in your heart to forgive her before it's too late."

"I think it already is, but I'll think about it," I said as I stood up.

"She'll do it when she's ready. Just give her time to process all of this," I heard my stepmom, Danielle, say to my father.

As I walked out the kitchen to go upstairs and get ready for my weekend with my girls, I decided I didn't have time to cry about a bitch that hadn't even been there for me my whole life. She made her choices and suddenly wanted to see me because she was on her deathbed. I could really give two fucks.

I packed my bags while periodically texting Jonathan and the girls. Before I knew it, I was passed out in my bed. When I woke up, I looked at my phone. I noticed four whole hours had passed since Lo told me she was on her way. I looked at all the missed calls I had from Tey and decided to call her back, but it went straight to voicemail.

I called Lo and the same thing happened, which caused me to become confused and wonder what the fuck was going on. Eventually, I got a call from a number I wasn't familiar with.

"Hello."

"Taj." Teyanna's voice cracked.

My heart began jumping out of my chest.

"Tey, what's going on?"

"Get to the hospital. It's bad. It's all bad." She began to hyperventilate while sobbing into the phone.

"What? What happened?" I stammered while throwing on my shoes and scrambling around my room for my jacket.

"It's Lo... I think she's dead," she cried harder and everything went blank.

After asking her what hospital, I grabbed my father's car keys without thinking twice and made my way to Mass General Hospital.

Chapter 31

Omniscient

Four hours earlier

"Alright, come on," Lo said, rushing him to get whatever he needed out the safe so they could get Taj and be on their merry way to NYC. She had already sent the text.

Bishop and Lo were at one of the many trap houses that Bishop and Terror owned in Boston. Lo had slowly but surely started learning more and more about the drug game. Bishop was shocked at how good she was when it came to counting money. Since he'd shown her how to use guns, Bishop felt like he had finally met the perfect match. Lo was a natural.

They couldn't get enough of each other. Lo was the only girl who hadn't pressured him to hand in his player's card. She told him that, when he was ready to take it seriously, she would be there. But, in the meantime, she was gon' do her too. Bishop loved that she was down and had his back when he felt nobody else did. They had the type of love that would be hard to break.

"Hold your little ass on. I told you that you could've waited in the car, but no, you wanted to come, so don't complain now." He closed the safe and made sure it was hidden before standing up and grabbing his lady's hand with one hand and the black Nike duffle bag in the other.

"Let's get a quickie in before we go get Taj's nosey ass," Bishop suggested while putting the duffle bag in the trunk and getting into the driver's side. Lo was spontaneous and down for whatever. When it came to Bishop, nothing was off limits. She laughed but knew he was dead serious.

"Maybe later. I told Taj we were on our way over a half-hour ago," she said while patting down her pockets.

"What's up, ma? What you looking for?"

"My phone; I think I left it in the house. I'll be back," she said, giving Bishop a quick peck before getting out the car and strutting into the house.

After five minutes, she still hadn't returned to the car, so Bishop decided to get out and go in the house to help. Before he could get all the way around the car, he saw a tall, shadowy figure run from the back of the house.

"What the fuck?" he mumbled with a puzzled look upon his face. One to shoot first and asks questions later, he pulled his .44 mag out the small of his back and turned the safety off. Once he was four feet away from the house, a big explosion went off, knocking Bishop a couple more feet away from the house and causing him to lose his handle on his gun.

Still dizzy, but frantic because his girl was still in the house, he staggered to his feet, not noticing someone with a .38 revolver behind him.

Bang!

The first shot ripped through Bishop's back. It was like everything went in slow motion as he turned around and faced the person that was trying to end his life.

He tried rushing toward the person holding the gun, but it was too late.

Bang!

He was shot again. This time in the right shoulder, which ripped right through him. Bishop was shocked, hurt, and angry all at the same time. As he felt himself become weaker, he dropped to his knees as the person walked closer and leveled the gun right in between his eyes.

A lady had come out of a house across the street and began screaming frantically as more neighbors came outside to see the havoc that had been done to their once quiet street. Hearing sirens in the distance, the shooter became scared and panicked, not paying attention to the target. They shot once more and grazed Bishop's head.

Bishop lay on the ground, bleeding out. As he felt himself become weaker and colder, he heard his car drive off.

Thinking about his love inside the house burning to death as he lost huge amounts of blood, he struggled to keep his eyes open as they became heavier. Once he heard the ambulance pull up, his heart rate slowed down tremendously.

He looked at the hand reaching for him and heard a familiar voice: his mother's.

"Come on, baby, momma's got you," he heard as he reached for her hand and took his last breath.

TO BE CONTINUED...

About The Author

Tana B was born in Boston, Massachusetts in the neighborhood of Dorchester on December 19th, 1995. Tana has lived in Springfield and Pittsfield, Massachusetts, where she began to write short stories. For the past five years, Tana B has been in Pittsfield, where she graduated from Taconic High School. Her first book, This Game Called Love, was in the Top 5 best sellers on Amazon and considered a National Bestseller. Tana has been recently writing the sequel to This Game Called Love as well as other stories in hopes of gaining more supporte and a stronger fan base.

Made in the USA
Monee, IL
04 September 2020

41251795R00072